PUBLIC LIBRARY

OCT 0 5 2012

ON

D1466682

NeWest
PRESS

Howard, B.
Western taxidermy.

PRICE: $19.95

SEP 2012

WESTERN TAXIDERMY

STORIES BY BARB HOWARD

NeWest
PRESS

Copyright © Barb Howard 2012

All rights reserved. The use of any part of this publication reproduced, transmitted in any form or by any means, electronic, mechanical, recording or otherwise, or stored in a retrieval system, without the prior consent of the publisher is an infringement of the copyright law. In the case of photocopying or other reprographic copying of the material, a licence must be obtained from Access Copyright before proceeding.

— — —

Library and Archives Canada Cataloguing in Publication

Howard, Barb, 1962–
Western Taxidermy / Barb Howard

Short Stories
Also issued in electronic format.
ISBN 978-1-927063-11-8
I. Title.

PS8586.0828W48 2012   C813'.6   C2011-906748-X

— — —

Editor for the Board: Anne Nothof
Cover and Interior Design: Greg Vickers
Author Photo: Boden/Ledingham Photography

NeWest Press acknowledges the financial support of the Alberta Multimedia Development Fund and the Edmonton Arts Council for our publishing program. We further acknowledge the financial support of the Government of Canada through the Canada Book Fund (CBF) for our publishing activities. We acknowledge the support of the Canada Council for the Arts which last year invested $24.3 million in writing and publishing throughout Canada.

201, 8540–109 Street
Edmonton, Alberta I T6G 1E6
780.432.9427
www.newestpress.com

NeWest Press

No bison were harmed in the making of this book.

We are committed to protecting the environment and to the responsible use of natural resources. This book was printed on 100% post-consumer recycled paper.

1 2 3 4 5 13 12 I Printed and bound in Canada

To my sister, Mary Howard, with love.

CONTENTS

WESTERN TAXIDERMY

Deirdre's mother opened the door when I arrived at the baby celebration. She reminded me of a monkey: short, with stringy limbs, close-set eyes, a wide, smiling mouth. Although, unlike a monkey, her face didn't have much expression. Too taut. Too shiny. Details you wouldn't notice if you weren't a taxidermist. But even with my training, at first glance I never would have guessed she was a grandmother. Primate, yes. Grandmother, yes.

She took my gift bag and set it down on the wicker bench with the other presents. "How very kind of you," she said, still smiling even though my bag, a reused wine sac closed with a piece of masking tape, stood out, in a bad way, from all the sunny floral-design bags spilling over with pastel paper and ribbon. She spent a few moments adjusting all the bags on the bench in order, it seemed, to camouflage mine under the tassels and tissues of others. Then she escorted me across the foyer and into the living room, where there was a bar. Not some impromptu card table with a Styrofoam cooler on top. This was a permanent bar with a sink and coasters and pink cocktail napkins and several bottles of white wine lined up and ready for consumption.

I wondered if Deirdre's mother was a bit loony. That would explain her peculiar looks and that non-stop smile. Everyone's got a loony somewhere in their family, I thought as she poured me a white wine, and hurrah for those families that let them out of the closet. She poured herself a diet pop.

Bob, Deirdre's husband, doesn't drink alcohol either. At least, I've never smelled booze on him. He is a sober hunter. I can sometimes tell if a hunter was drunk in the field. Ragged cuts, wet cape, broken antlers. Admittedly, with the increasing number of hunters who don't know a thing about field care, it's getting harder to tell who was drunk and who is just ignorant.

"Cheers," Deirdre's mother said, holding her glass up to me.

"Cheers," I said and downed the wine right away so I wouldn't have to carry the glass around with me. I'm practical that way.

Deirdre's mother steered me, bordering on a push really, towards a cluster of women near the fireplace.

They were talking about back fat. I stood close to them, pretending to admire the river rock mantel—which would have been a perfect location for a 360° pheasant mount—so I could hear what they were talking about.

"It's just so horrible," one woman was saying, "to think that it's there, behind you, where everyone but you can see it."

"I'm Kay," I interrupted. "I heard you talking about back fat. In taxidermy we peel back the skin and use a deflesher to scrape the fat. Maybe that's what you need."

"Maybe," she said, dabbing at her mouth with her pink napkin, even though she hadn't eaten anything.

The rest of the women were silent.

I shook all their hands, taking care not to squeeze too tightly on the fingers with big rings. I didn't want to hurt these women. They hadn't done anything to me.

I saw Deirdre on the other side of the room. Her mother had moved in beside her and they were talking closely. I waved. I had indirectly met Deirdre before; it was the first time Bob came to my shop. They had seen my business sign and Bob decided to stop in for a look. Deirdre never even got out of the car, but she was memorable. Her hair was done like a lion's pelt. It was the same at the baby celebration, maybe even a bit lighter, more of an anemic lion. I know quite a bit about hair and I can tell you, there wasn't a natural pelt at the party. Some of the hair in the room was positively alien. Deirdre's mother's, for instance. She had black hair. Completely black, not a hint of reflection or variation. Trust me, there is no creature on this planet with natural hair that black. At a taxidermy competition, you would never see hair like that on a blue ribbon mount.

Deirdre wore a high-necked sweater that clung to her

big boobs. Not stupidly big boobs, like the woman with the cocktail laugh who was setting out lamb appetizers and relocating the gifts to the coffee table. No, Deirdre's boobs were within the realm of recessive genetic possibility. One look at those breasts and you knew that Bob, her husband, must be a breast man. Which was news to me. He told me he was a leg man. I was wearing shorts, cutoffs, at the time. I do have good coltish legs.

Deirdre's boobs didn't seem to have that hard-looking bloat from breast-feeding, or those long dog-nipples that you sometimes see on female animals. I've always hated it when someone brings a postpartum animal into my shop. They are usually roadkill, since hunting seasons avoid nursing times. But accidents happen, or laws are broken, and the babies left behind don't have a chance. Bob would never bring down a nursing mother. He told me so.

I excused myself from the silent back fat women and crossed the room to chat with Deirdre. First I had to mingle my way through a small satellite group that surrounded her. Her mother had disappeared.

"Kay Holmes," I said, holding out my hand.

"Nice to meet you," said the first woman whose hand I shook. "We're just talking about cosmoplast. Did you know it comes from foreskin stem cells?"

"Deirdre's just had an injection and she looks fantastic," the next woman said.

"I've been meaning to get some cosmoplast," I said. "In taxidermy, wrinkles can be a real issue. You only want them where they're supposed to be, like on old animals and anuses."

"No doubt," the first women said.

"My dad, my mentor, said we can never get too comfortable in our trade. We need to keep learning so we can keep earning," I added, but the woman had turned her back to me, leaving me a clear line to Deirdre.

Deirdre was wearing suede pants with a beautiful nap. Brand new, judging from the lack of wear. Rurban acreage people like Deirdre like to do their own version of western wear. Cropped jackets with fringe, three-quarter sleeve form-fit shirts, tight leather pants, miniature platinum horseshoes on their ears, maybe two on each ear. I call it "western shrink wrap" and refuse to participate. In honour of the baby celebration, I was wearing a khaki-coloured blouse, even though I hate the slippery material, and I had pressed my jeans.

"Here's Kay. She's a taxidermist," Deirdre said, by way of introducing me as I budged into her inner circle. "Isn't that wild?"

"I couldn't stand it. All those poor animals," one woman said.

"I'm a vegetarian," another one said. "Except for salmon. You're supposed to eat salmon."

"Kay's a great friend of Bob's," Deirdre said. "A great, great friend."

"Congratulations on the baby," I said. "Is she around?"

"Down there." Deirdre pointed towards a wide hallway

with several doorways on each side. Sort of like a shopping mall.

I hadn't been to a baby shower in a decade. Not since high school, when Holly Tompkins got pregnant in Grade 12 and her mother cried and served devilled eggs for the duration of the party. I live a pretty isolated life in my shop; most of my clients are middle-aged males, and I've never really done the female group thing. Just not a herd animal, I guess. The only reason I was invited to this shower was because I had called to leave a message for Bob to say that his bear would be ready by the weekend. Deirdre answered his cell phone and, since Bob had mentioned that he was going to be a father, I said congratulations. Deirdre said come over that afternoon, there was a party at her house, for her and the baby. They weren't calling it a shower; it was a baby celebration. Even though I live forty-five minutes away, she said I was like a neighbour, I must come, I was such a good friend of Bob's. He was always talking about me, she said. He'd love to know that she and I had finally spent some time together.

I bet he would. And I bet Deirdre would love to make a hillbilly of me at her celebration. So I spent the morning doing up a few invoices on the computer, put together a gift, and took the afternoon off. I could even justify it as client appreciation. Deirdre's husband Bob is my favourite. He always prepares his animals properly in the field, always pays on time, in cash, and always pays me a compliment. For instance, when I work in my shop, which is attached to my house, I wear a short canvas apron over my clothes. Bob says he likes the way the apron sits snug around my hips and waist. He calls it my French maid taxidermy outfit.

As I walked down the hall looking for the baby, I passed various bedrooms and a den, and then a massive bathroom where Deirdre's mother was applying a topcoat of creamy red lipstick.

"I suppose you're wondering where your work is," she said, turning my way. "Wonder where he puts it all?"

"Oh no," I said. "Not at all. I was looking for the baby."

"Well, I guess Bob won't be hunting much now that he and Deirdre have a baby."

"I know lots of men who keep hunting once they have children. Some bring their kids along."

"Perhaps," Deirdre's mother said slowly, "I'm not making myself clear. Bob is devoted to Deirdre."

Under other circumstances, I might have laughed. But even though Deirdre's mother's facial features were in the exact same position as when she had opened the front door for me, still smiling, not a wrinkle or furrow in sight, something about her eyes made her seem predatory. Good hunters have warned me: stay away from overprotective mothers. I thought it best to simply respond to her with a small nod of my head that meant absolutely nothing.

"You're not convinced," she said. "The trophy room is downstairs. You must see it. I'll take you there. We can pick up the baby on our way back."

The trophy room was a mess. I could make out a desk, beautiful quarter-cut oak, covered in magazines and papers and dead computer equipment. On top of everything was the bull elk—head and shoulders—I had mounted for Bob two years ago. On the floor, mixed in with a pair of heavy winter boots, was the moose mount from the year he got his moose tag, and the little pronghorn he had caught stateside. The pronghorn was my first project for him—a pedestal mount. Everything I had done for Bob, five hunting seasons' worth of work, was junked in this room.

"That Bob," Deirdre's mother said, putting her hands on her hips. "Tut, tut. He should take better care of your work."

I blew dust off the forehead of the pronghorn. The way Bob treated my work was a surprise to me. He was always praising my taxidermy, as he should, because I am good at it. My father and grandfather ran Western Taxidermy before I inherited it. I have all their skill, and then some.

Deirdre's mother was watching me. Her smile might have been real. She was good at this sort of thing. She knew she had caught me off guard.

"Doesn't matter to me," I said. "As long as I get paid. Maybe Bob just likes the hunt."

On the way back from the trophy room, Deirdre's mother turned through the doorway of a pink bedroom where a sulky teenage girl sat reading a beauty magazine. The crib, containing a baby, was beside her. I looked into the crib and discovered that the baby was nice and fat, with a bit of acne on her forehead. Not unlike the teenage girl.

"This is Megan. One of the guests' daughters," Roxanna said. "Charging us an outrageous eight bucks an hour to sit with the baby."

Megan continued to read the magazine. Deirdre's mother picked up the baby and kissed her, leaving a red lipstick smear on the baby's cheek. Then she pulled the baby up to her shoulder. I got a look at Deirdre's mother's hands. They were thick and liver-spotted with beautifully painted nails. I do a bit of painting myself. Oil paint and a traditional brush for noses, gums, that sort of thing. Airbrushing for the interiors of ears. So I know fine work. But what most fascinated me, especially from my professional point of view, was the way Deirdre's mother's old painted hands were juxtaposed with her smooth face. She was like a taxidermy novelty piece. A jackalope.

When Deirdre's mother and the baby and I came into the living room, the woman with the stupidly big breasts called for everyone to sit around the coffee table. Deirdre sat down in a high-backed chair. I sat a few seats down from her. Deirdre's mother sat next to me.

"Any trips lately?" one of the women asked her.

"Oh yes," Deirdre's mother said. "A safari to South Africa."

She handed me the baby. Then she stood up, held her arms in the air and slowly twirled once to show the other women her monkey body. I adjusted the baby in my arms, tried to get the knack of holding the bundle and rocking to and fro to keep the baby from whimpering, while Deirdre's mother went on talking. "I went with Dr. Mentos' group again. We saw the big five."

"Were you hunting?" I asked because I knew the big five: leopard, cheetah, Cape buffalo, elephant, and white rhino. Years ago, when my dad did taxidermy, hunters went to Africa to try and bag them all. My job was to make bottle openers out of claws.

"Oh God, no. It was a surgery safari. My third, actually. This year I had a breast lift and a bit of lipo, and then went and saw the animals with the rest of the women. Next year Deirdre is going to come with me."

The baby's perfect little fingers reached out of the blanket. The women on either side of me were oohing over the baby and whispering to each other about the gifts they had brought. Store-bought layette sets and leather booties and pink jean jackets and a teeny charm bracelet with coordinating earrings. Nothing like I had brought. I knew that I should be passing the baby around but I didn't. I wanted to hug her and let her know that I liked her, nothing was her fault, she had never done anything to embarrass me. The present I had brought was really for her mother.

After opening all the other gifts, Deirdre peeled off the masking tape and reached her hand into the wine bag I had brought. She pulled out my offering and her white smile sagged. I had prepared a gopher. I had run over it a few weeks ago when I backed my truck out of my garage. Its bones were crushed, but its exterior was relatively unmarred. I tossed it in the freezer. When Deirdre invited me to the celebration, I thawed the gopher in the microwave, turned it inside out, scraped it clean, and stuffed it the old-fashioned way, with cotton batting. Then I posed it to stand on its back legs, the cute way gophers do sometimes when they stand near their homes. I finished up the details: nails, nose, eyes, teeth to give it a cute, inquisitive look. Sure, it was no Robert Bateman, but it was pretty good given my time constraints.

"Did you make this?" Deirdre asked.

Everyone, including Deirdre, kept looking at the gopher instead of at me.

"Sure. It's more of a knick-knack than a plaything," I said.

Deirdre flattened the wine bag on the table and then, using only her thumb and index finger, set the gopher on the bag. She didn't pass it around the circle of women. Someone reached over the back of my chair and plucked the baby from my arms. The celebration was over.

Back at my shop, I've got a lot of work to do. Verna Harding caught a tyee on the West Coast that her husband wants mounted for a Christmas present. It was catch and release, so I have to construct the whole fish based on a photo and measurements. I hate doing fish. Then there's McCullough's mule deer to finish. Lovely buck. Except that McCullough kept it in his freezer for half a year before bringing it to me. The freezer burn caused me no end of alignment problems.

And then there's Bob's bear. I've done a particularly realistic job on that bear. The tanned skin was easy to work with. I took great care to set the facial features properly and turn out a high-quality felt-backed rug for him. But I've decided to make a few alterations. Forget realism for Bob. I'm going to pull the bear's head skin over the armature until it looks ready to tear. I'm going to give it thick, curly eyelashes and unnaturally streaked hair and neon white teeth and maybe even a set of saline teats. Then my work will get displayed in his living room.

BIG FORK PLAYGROUND

"We'll be incommunicado for weeks," Craig says, studying a topo map from his place in the passenger seat. "Several multi-pitch climbs are on the agenda."

Jeanie isn't bothered that she is neither invited nor involved in the trans-Rockies trek he has planned for later in the summer. After all, she knows that Craig, besides being a legendary outdoorsman, is a bit of an asshole. Her co-worker Marilyn, who got them together, said "You'll love him—he's really good-looking" so many times that Jeanie knew there must be something up with his personality. But Jeanie wanted to go camping, she wanted to see what Westitch clients found so enthralling, and when she met Craig she knew he was just the person to initiate her—even if it was only for one night at Big Fork. Craig said that was all the "car camping" he could stand. Jeanie said that was all the time she could afford away from her job and mother.

As they drive into Big Fork, Craig folds his map, grimaces out the window.

"Look at the yahoos," he says. "Why don't they just stay at home if they're going to plug in a generator and roll out a fake lawn?"

"Maybe it's the idea of not being home. You know, when you're home you've got a lot of stuff to do."

"I don't. Why not stay in a hotel?"

"They couldn't bring their miniature dogs."

"Those dogs—they're an embarrassment to their species. Drive over them."

"Kill them?" Jeanie asks.

"Absolutely. Do the world a favour." Craig opens his window, cranes his neck. "Sweet Jeezus, they've even got a caretaker here. How badly would that job suck?"

Jeanie, trying to avoid the dogs scampering around the car, doesn't turn to look at the caretaker. At the end of the last loop in the campground, having long outpaced the dogs, she spots the green Volvo. Jeanie's co-worker Marilyn, with her partner Wayne, came out earlier in the day to reserve the campsite. Jeanie parks beside their Volvo.

Wayne runs to Jeanie's car. He reaches his arm through the open passenger window and pumps Craig's hand.

"Craig!" Wayne says. "Craig," he says again, calming himself. "I bet Marilyn that you'd never come on this hokey trip."

"One night only," Craig says.

"I'm with you there," Wayne says. "Oh, hi Jeanie."

Wayne always enrolls in Craig's classes on backcountry skills. Jeanie has met Wayne several times before, but he never acknowledges her unless she is with Craig. That, Jeanie supposes, is because she is not the outdoors type. Craig once called her a cubicle babe. But stockbroker Wayne, at least physically, hardly looks the backcountry type himself.

"Welcome to our backyard," Marilyn calls from the picnic table. She wears her usual: braids, toque, and Westitch clothing. Nobody uses their employee discount to greater advantage than Marilyn, who works in the retail department.

"May as well be the city," Craig mutters.

"It all seems pretty nice to me," Jeanie says, gesturing to the fir trees, the fire pit, the rustic picnic table, and the tent. "Is that your tent? It looks so small."

"There's room to set yours up on the other side of the fire pit," Marilyn says.

Craig spreads his map on one end of the picnic table and begins to show Marilyn and Wayne his summer plans. Jeanie unloads the car, making several trips for all Craig's gear. When she picked up Craig earlier in the afternoon, she discovered that true campers pack in little nylon sacks. He must have had ten of them. She, on the other hand, crammed everything into a gym bag, except her duvet, which she carried directly from her bed to her hatchback. Craig was shocked that Jeanie, the comptroller of Westitch Outdoor Co., didn't have a sleeping bag.

But why would she have a sleeping bag? Westitch hired her for her ability with numbers, not to test equipment.

She piles Craig's nylon sacks on the other end of the picnic table. Watches for a few moments as Marilyn focuses on rebraiding her hair and Wayne unsuccessfully tries to get himself invited on Craig's trek.

"The tent?" Jeanie asks.

"In a minute," Craig answers, sliding his pinky finger from the scale bar and across the map to calculate distances.

It helps that Craig is good-looking. Very Craig-y, especially where his cheeks sink in above his jaw. Some people, like Marilyn, find that his looks alone offset his selfishness. But Jeanie finds his selfishness, in and of itself, strangely appealing. Other than a loose pocket of male acquaintances and an intermittent job, he has no bonds. No parents to take care of, definitely no dying mother who combined the self-effacing roles of single mother and palliative care nurse for almost forty years.

Eventually Craig closes the map and pulls retractable poles and nylon fabric from the tiniest sack on the table. He spreads the material across from Marilyn and Wayne's tent and inserts the poles. In a few moments he has set up a white, low-profile tent. It looks like a body bag.

"What now?" Jeanie asks, clapping her hands together.

"Jeanie, you are such a micro-manager," Marilyn says in mock exasperation. "Do you ever relax?"

"I'm relaxing," Jeanie says. "I'm camping. How about some wood?"

The other three look confused.

"I saw it stacked up near the entrance. Five bucks a

bundle," Jeanie says.

"We have stoves," Wayne says. "Craig probably has a really good stove."

"Campfires are for Girl Guides," Craig adds. "Not to mention bad for the environment."

Jeanie looks at the fire pit. She never was a Girl Guide. But her mother, forever patient, forever smiling, taught her how to make a fire when they went on picnics. Jeanie knows how to prop the kindling into the shape of a hermit's cabin. Then stick a match through the door-hole and watch the empty house go up in flames.

"Isn't the fire pit for fires?" Jeanie asks.

"Do what you like," Craig says, shrugging. "But I'm not cooking on it."

Jeanie walks back to the entrance of the campground. The bundles of wood are flanked by several metres of plastic lawn leading to a trailer. Directly in front of the trailer there is a man sprawled on an old car seat that serves as a couch. He's watching a football game on television under the protection of a huge tarped canopy.

When Jeanie nears the wood, the man hops off the car seat and approaches her. He is sixtyish, pot-bellied, wearing baggy jeans. The name tag pinned to his checked shirt reads: "Caretaker."

"Wood?" Jeanie asks, pulling a ten-dollar bill from her pocket.

"Why doesn't that fella you drove in with come and carry the wood himself?" the caretaker asks.

"He doesn't want a fire."

"He's a backcountry prick. I knew it. The rangers tell me it costs more to rescue a backcountry prick than it does to maintain a full-service campground for the season."

"I think he knows what he's doing."

"Let 'em die, I say. Here, borrow my wheelbarrow. May as well take my axe for the night, too. Can't split wood with lover boy's fruit leather."

Back at the campsite, Jeanie makes a hermit's house in the fire pit, while Craig works on unfolding and lighting his compact stove. He sets a miniature pot of water on to boil.

"Thanks for taking on dinner, Craig," Marilyn says. "What's cooking?"

"Succotash stew," Craig answers, waving a foil bag at them. "I'm test driving it for my summer trek."

"Perfect," Wayne says.

Jeanie has been hoping for hot dogs and marshmallows. Maybe only Girl Guides eat those things. And beans. What about a can of baked beans? That's what she and her mother would cook on a fire. And her mother would tell stories about her work on the palliative ward. The stories, Jeanie knew from a young age, were meant to inspire her towards a life of compassionate duty.

Jeanie decides to contribute to the dinner by hosting cocktail hour. She returns to the car and zips open the gym bag. Snuggled inside her long underwear and a spare oversized sweater, she has packed several bottles of wine. More wine than she imagined they'd ever drink, but she wasn't sure who liked red or white or, now that she thought about it, which would go better with freeze-dried succotash.

"Booze?" Craig looks incredulously at the bottles in her arms.

"Wine."

"You brought booze?" Wayne echoes.

"Bring it on," Marilyn laughs.

Jeanie uncorks a bottle. Three mugs, including Craig's, appear on the table.

"Anybody got a mug for me?" Jeanie asks.

Craig hands her a plastic measuring cup.

Craig's stove continues to fail, and by the time the third bottle is opened, cocktail hour has stretched from an hour to an endurance event. Jeanie takes breaks from the wine while she tends the fire and chops wood.

"Just sit still," Marilyn says when Jeanie pulls another log from the wheelbarrow. "Tell us about yourself. Chat."

"Myself?" Jeanie asks.

"Okay, tell us about your mother," Marilyn prompts. "You're always leaving work to go and see her. How's she doing?"

Jeanie fusses with the log, trying to get it to stand on end, ready for chopping, wondering if Marilyn's question is actually a dig at how often she leaves work. Probably not. Nobody could criticize Jeanie for not working hard enough. Especially Marilyn. But it is true that every day, sometimes twice a day, she leaves Westitch to drive to the nursing home to help her mother eat. The nurses say that her mother won't eat the pureed servings unless Jeanie does the feeding. Craig says the nurses are just trying to make Jeanie feel good about herself, and that her mother probably doesn't know or care who is spooning in the gruel.

Jeanie begins, "My mother has an inoperable brain tumour. At this stage, she can't speak. Or move much."

"Why doesn't she just die?" Craig interrupts. He is lying on the bench beside the picnic table, frequently propping himself up to check the feeble stove flame.

"No kidding," Wayne says.

"That's an awful way to talk," Marilyn says, then refills her mug with wine. "No wonder Jeanie looks so pale and harassed. Good wine, by the way."

Jeanie takes a swing at the log.

"Nursing homes make me gag," Craig says.

Eventually, Craig distributes parsimonious servings of lukewarm stew.

"Succotash," Marilyn giggles, having had her fair share of wine. "Sufferin' shuckatosh."

"Brilliant," Wayne says after a quick taste.

Craig has moved from the picnic table to the fire. He squats, holding his tin dish of succotash between his knees. "This is shitty," he decides after a few spoonfuls. "I'm not taking it on my trip."

Jeanie sniffs her bowl, disappointed because she is so hungry. The yellow stew smells like formaldehyde. She stirs the stew around, gaining courage to eat. It's not like a crummy dinner will kill her. Her mother has to eat meals that look like this all the time and, for whatever reason, she's still alive. Before she brings the spoon to her mouth, Jeanie feels a shadow move over her. She glances up and sees a fast-moving black blanket of cloud taking over the sky.

"Mountain weather rolling in," Craig announces. The effort of tilting his head back makes him lose his balance and topple. He spills the remainder of his stew on his polypropylene shirt.

Jeanie has never seen such a quick turn in the sky, although she has heard about the unpredictability of mountain weather. Craig lies on the ground, apparently in no hurry to move. Marilyn and Wayne are playing kissyface and spooning succotash into each other's mouths.

Jeanie picks up the empty wine bottles and carries them to a recycling bin in the parking lot. She closes Craig's stove and seals the fuel bottle. Then she does a quick rinse of everyone's dishes before telescoping them together and putting them in her car.

From there, she spots the outhouse and hurries for a visit before the hail starts. While she pees, the outhouse darkens as though someone has dimmed the lights. By the time she returns to the campsite, she almost needs a flashlight even though it is still early evening. Marilyn, Wayne, and Craig have gone into the tents for cover.

Jeanie crawls into Craig's tent. She stops to let her eyes, and nasal passages, adjust to the darkness and to the reek of succotash farts. Craig is sprawled across his sleeping bag and her duvet. Jeanie starts to crawl into the narrow space on one side of the tent. As she moves forward, Craig pulls her on top of him. He exhales wine and succotash and formaldehyde. She turns her head to one side.

They roll awkwardly over, hitting the wall of the tent. Craig kisses Jeanie's cheek, her chin, her neck, and then stalls near her collarbone. Jeanie gives him an encouraging peck on the top of his head. After all, he's moving in the right direction. He kisses her collarbone, sinks his face into her chest. At first she thinks he is sniffing her, perhaps some sort of inhalation thing that might be sexy, but then she realizes, by his deep steady breathing and lack of progress, that Craig has passed out.

Jeanie pushes him away and listens as the first burst of hail begins outside. It smacks against the tent like a drum roll. Once in a while there is a pinging sound as a ball of hail hits a tent pole and ricochets into the campsite.

When the hail lightens to a soft rain, Jeanie can hear Marilyn and Wayne arguing in their tent. Wayne wants children. He says he will do more than his share of parenting. Their voices rise.

"Which part of 'no' are you not understanding?" Marilyn asks.

"Just one kid," Wayne says. "Someone to take care of us in our old age."

"That's stupid," Marilyn scoffs. "Look at poor Jeanie."

Jeanie lies back, studies the water droplets and tree silhouettes on the other side of the thin nylon fabric. The ground is probably soaked. No sense trying to restart the fire now. Nothing else to do but go back to bed. No mother. No job. No duty. Car camping, Jeanie decides as she yanks her duvet from underneath Craig, is lovely.

In the morning, everyone except Jeanie is grumpy.

"Don't bother with the stove," Craig snaps. "Let's just get a move on."

"Breakfast?" Jeanie asks.

"I'm not running a restaurant. There are protein bars in the car," Craig answers.

"What's the rush?"

"The sooner I'm out of here, the better," Craig says.

"Go ahead," Jeanie urges. "Go back with Wayne and Marilyn."

By the way they are punching their sleeping bags into stuff sacks beside the tent, Jeanie can tell that Wayne and Marilyn have a fight to finish at home.

"You wouldn't mind?" Craig asks, perking up considerably.

"Not at all. I'll hang around and take the tents down after they've had a chance to dry." Jeanie hopes it sounds as though she is driven by kindness and martyrdom. Really, she just wants to be rid of them all.

"You're a saint," Craig says.

Craig, Marilyn and Wayne load their belongings into the Volvo. Wayne starts the car and begins to back away from the campsite. The car stops abruptly. Craig hops out carrying a nylon stuff sack in his hand.

"Here, protein bars in case you get hungry," he says.

"Thanks," Jeanie says. There must be sixty bars in the bag. How long does he think she is going to stay here by herself? A month? Now there's a thought.

Craig fishes around in the bag. He pulls out a Frontier Fudge bar, his favourite flavour, and tosses the bag on the picnic table. Maybe Craig's not just an asshole with a tent, Jeanie thinks as she watches him jog back to the Volvo. Maybe he's got everything figured out.

Before she can pick a bar for herself out of the bag, she hears a clinking of bottles and then another motor, not the Volvo. Jeanie turns to see the caretaker, in his checked shirt and jeans, riding a quad. Behind the quad he tows a small trailer containing Jeanie's empty wine bottles. He drives into the campsite and right up to Jeanie.

"Just picked up your recyclables. That's a lot of dead soldiers. Must've been quite a party last night. Are you staying on alone?"

"Thinking about it." Jeanie looks at the tents and the bag of power bars.

"I'll bring you a load of wood after I dump these bottles," the caretaker says, revving his engine. He pops the front tires in the air and wheelies back to the main road, leaving her alone.

After Jeanie watches the caretaker drive away, she takes inventory. Here at Big Fork she has food, shelter and a caretaker. All the necessities of life.

MY BROTHER'S SHIT-KICKERS

My big brother Tom wore snakeskin shit-kickers. Not just the uppers; the whole boot, except the sole and heel, was shimmering reptile. Whenever he bought a new pair he'd want me to run my hands along the scaly material.

"Genuine snakeskin. Feel that, kid," he said to me once when we were watching television. He swung his leg up so that his cowboy boot rested on my lap.

I cringed into the couch, but brushed the tips of my fingers along the pointy toe.

"How can you appreciate that material? You're hardly touching it."

"Snakes give me the willies," I admitted.

"Grab a hold. Right there at the instep."

I held my breath and grasped his boot with both hands.

"Look out!" my brother yelled, jerking his foot in the

air. "It's alive."

I shrieked, jumped. While my brother laughed and laughed, I left the room to call my best friend Cindy.

Talking to Cindy comprised the most important portion of my day. A half-hour after we walked home from school we would phone each other with updates. If my brother was home when the phone rang, he would give me the "challenge eye"—a slight rise of his eyebrows and a sideways glance, and then he'd race me to the phone. I tried my hardest to beat him because his responses to Cindy were stupid and humiliating. "You'll have to call back. Diane's busy walking around naked and complaining that there's a crack in her butt." Despite his telephone manner, Cindy phoned even more frequently when Tom was home.

My brother worked the rigs. Three weeks in, three weeks out. When he was away, I had the phone to myself. I had my Mom to myself. We would have small feminine meals. Open-faced sandwiches and instant Spring Vegetable soup. Or canned pineapple rings on cottage cheese. Sometimes Cindy would stay for supper. She complained about her horrible younger siblings and the atrocities committed at mealtime at her house. My Mom smiled at Cindy's complaints.

"You have no idea how bad it is," Cindy wailed. "Never sophisticated like this. Our kitchen is like a food fair."

"Things will change, honey," Mom assured her.

"Not in my lifetime," Cindy mumbled.

"Things will change" was also my mother's response to

any angst I was feeling about school or friends. Like Cindy, I found it an unhelpful comment. Left to ourselves, both Cindy and I would mimic my Mom's smile and nod, and pat each other on the head saying, "Things will change," and then giggle a list of affectionate names. "Sweetest pie, honey pot, garlic breath, bum face, fart head."

Mom cooked. I did the dishes. We slept in side-by-side rooms upstairs. We left the house at the same time in the morning—she to her editing job, me to school. We arrived home at about the same time. We folded laundry together. By the end of three weeks we were bored and snippy with each other. Our talk began to revolve around Tom's expected arrival. My Mom recited meaty meals, perhaps a rump roast or sloppy joes, that she planned to cook for dinner. I suggested errands that Tom and I could do for my Mom— because I loved to be in his little red car.

By the time Tom arrived, even a walk down the front steps to his Toyota seemed exciting. In the summer he might fire his car keys at me. "Think fast, kid." I never had to think so fast that I couldn't catch the keys. In the winter, the smooth sole of his cowboy boots caused him to slip, yelp, run a few steps, but never crash. Any season, if I was in the passenger seat, Tom would pull his Toyota into my empty school parking lot and demonstrate donuts and brake stands. I loved the rush of spinning in circles or careening past the teachers' parking blocks.

If we drove by my friends, especially Cindy, Tom would recline his seat and drive with his shit-kickers, his long skinny legs pretzelled between his head and the steering wheel. The radio would be cranked, 1140 CKXL blasting top ten hits from the car to the sidewalk.

"I wish I could come with you and your brother sometime," Cindy pleaded.

"We just go for groceries."

"I could sit in the back seat. I could meet you at your house—like, you wouldn't have to come and pick me up or anything."

"I don't know. You wouldn't tell your mother?"

"I swear to God."

"I don't know. The back seat's pretty small."

Before my brother left for each shift, my Mom delivered her familiar lecture. She never bugged him about finishing school, but she had plenty of safety advice. Usually she began when she came through the door, as though she had been withholding her words all day at work.

"Get yourself a truck," Mom said, hanging her purse on the back of a kitchen chair. "A sturdy North American truck. I'll help you pay for it. You can't keep driving that matchbox to the drill sites." She put her hands on her hips and stood in front of Tom. "Get yourself a hard hat. And wear it. Get yourself out of there if they're not following procedures. If they're letting you wear those cowpoke boots, they're not following procedures."

Tom kept nodding and saying "Yep, yep, yep." He rolled his eyes at me. Mom poked two fingers into his chest.

"Listen up. This is important."

Tom fell on the floor, writhing, feigning a mortal wound at the site of the two-finger poke. Mom slid her hands into her pantsuit pockets and dropped her shoulders. I stepped on Tom's stomach on my way to the cupboard for a chocolate-dipped Wagon Wheel.

My brother didn't phone ahead when he finished a shift. He just drove home and walked into the house. His boots clicked across the slate at our front door.

"That'll be your brother," my Mom would say, patting the enamel sailboat that hung at her neck. My brother had given her that sailboat, which looked more like an umbrella to me, when he was a little boy. None of us had ever been sailing.

"Tom, you take those cowboy boots off," she'd shout from the kitchen, then, listening to the uninterrupted click of heels on the slate, she'd hustle to the front door. "Now!"

"Can't," he'd say, as he stepped off the slate and headed up the carpeted stairs that led to his room. "Can't get them off."

I half believed him. I knew he must take them off to sleep and shower. But in my twelve years, I couldn't recall him without cowboy boots.

"Hogwash," my Mom would say. "They're scratching the slate. I paid a fortune for that slate."

"Got to buy them tight," he'd say, "otherwise they'll get sloppy."

When my Mom got to the stairs, she gave him the two-finger poke. "You're not in some boondocks trailer," she'd say.

"I'm sure not," he'd say.

"You're sure not," she'd say, putting her arms around his waist and hugging him so tight her face squashed against his chest.

Tom was usually home for more than three weeks during spring thaw because the ground became too soft for the heavy vehicles used in drilling. When he came home, the snow would be melting from our yard, revealing the underlying dog shit. We didn't have a pet, but our neighbour's dog favoured our yard. Shortly after Tom arrived home, he would start the lawn work. I spectated while he lined the point of his boot up, took a step back, then, arms out, hopped forward and punted a lump of dog shit all the way to the curb or into the hedge.

"Use a shovel," Mom would laugh. "Diane, get him a shovel."

Occasionally, Tom kicked a shit onto our neighbour's roof. "Whoopsy," he would say loudly.

A few days before my thirteenth birthday, we heard the front door swing open and the familiar click of boots across the slate. My Mom and I had been making cheese popcorn—I had talked her into watching a horror movie on TV. Cindy had to babysit her siblings, otherwise I would have asked her to sleep over and watch the movie with us.

"Just putting my bag away." Tom embraced my Mom with his free hand, rested his chin on her head for a few moments. He winked at me. "Hello kid."

I wished I had been wearing my birthday present—a red smock top. I had already seen it—in fact, I had picked it out at Fairweather—but Mom had wrapped it up, to be opened only on my official birthday in a few days. Everyone wore smock tops at school. Even though Mom complained that they looked like maternity blouses, she bought me one.

I said, "Hi." I felt pleased that Cindy was at her own house.

"Think fast." The Toyota keys sailed towards my head.

My birthday fell during spring breakup and, at least for the few years since he had quit school to work, I could count on my brother for an extravagant gift. For my eleventh birthday he gave me a portable tape recorder and a couple of cassettes, including the Stampeders. Even better, for my twelfth birthday he gave me an electric vanity mirror and a bag of Bonne Bell cosmetics. Now Cindy and I could see ourselves made up, in movie star lights, singing the Stampeders' "Devil You." I suspected that Cindy imagined herself singing to my brother.

Once when Cindy stayed for dinner, my brother leaned back in his chair and plopped his booted foot on his place mat. "Look at that boot, Cindy," he said. "That heel's not just glued on. It's nailed up and down."

Cindy blushed, then giggled.

"For Pete's sake," I said after dinner, when Cindy and I were sharing a cigarette behind the utility box in the alley, "he's my brother."

Cindy, much more bold in Tom's absence, said, "He's a

hunk. A hunka hunka. And I love those boots."

"His boots are gross."

Cindy rounded her lips and tapped her cheek so that a series of tiny smoke rings pumped out of her mouth.

"He's not a cowboy, Cindy. The only time he's ever ridden a horse he was scared to death. He should be wearing hiking boots or Adidas like everyone else."

The night before my thirteenth birthday, I heard my brother's footsteps, unusually light and quick, as he ran upstairs to his bedroom. I pulled back my covers, peeked into the hall. I saw Tom crouch to adjust a white bow on a stuffed pink mouse. The mouse was huge, bigger than my brother's torso. Flat plastic eyes and two plush yellow teeth made it appear mechanical, or maniacal—anything but cute. More remarkable than the mouse, however, were two shimmering spots at the end of my brother's jeans. His bare feet. They were short and round, with plump little toes, and a whiteness, an incredible whiteness that made them look phosphorescent against the dark carpet.

I could not remember ever seeing my brother's bare feet. I must have assumed that they looked like his shit-kickers. Long, with crinkled leathery skin covering bent-up bones. But Tom's feet had skin like Cindy's baby sister's.

Not noticing me, my brother picked up the mouse, then took the stairs down, three or four at a time. I snuck back into my bed and held my arms over my tensing stomach. I was almost thirteen. I had a pack of Craven A menthol cigarettes in my closet. Cindy and I were seriously considering buying a bag of weed from a kid in grade nine. I was going to a bonfire party on the weekend.

A stuffed mouse. What was my brother thinking?

The next morning, my birthday, I stayed in my room well past breakfast time. I listened to the voices of my Mom and Tom in the kitchen. The scratch of a chair. I heard my Mom turn on the radio on the kitchen counter. Eventually I pulled a sweatshirt over my pyjamas and followed the smell of beef breakfast strips to the kitchen. There, on the centre of the table, beside my wrapped smock top, was the big stuffed mouse. Even before I entered the kitchen my Mom caught my eye. She smiled encouragingly at the mouse and then at me. "Happy birthday, Sweetheart."

My brother was at the kitchen table. "How 'bout this, kid?" He grabbed the fuzzy front feet and two-stepped the mouse towards me.

"Wow. That's great," I said, flipping the mouse's ears inside out. "Thanks."

"I'm heading out to the mall to pick up a few things. Come for a ride?" my brother asked. He tossed the car keys at me. "C'mon, kid. You start the car." The keys smacked on the table.

"No thanks."

"You go along," Mom said to Tom.

"I'll shower first," Tom said.

Tom left the kitchen and my Mom brought a glass of orange juice to the table. She sat beside me. "You did a good job." She put her arm around me. "So did Tom. Everybody's different. It's hard to know what sort of gift a person would want."

I worked at swallowing my sip of juice.

"There, there." She stroked my head until I sobbed, "I'm thirteen. Not a baby," and turned my head into her shoulder to cry.

"Things will change, Sweet Pea."

Tom returned to the kitchen after his shower. I was dry-eyed and eating cereal. His wet hair dripped on his white Levi's shirt.

"Hey, kid, you wearing your pyjamas or the new maternity shirt?" Tom asked, wiping a trickle of water from his neck.

"Don't call it that," Mom said. "It's a smock top. And don't call her kid."

"Can I still start your car?" I asked, setting down my spoon.

Tom dropped the keys out of his hand, caught them with the toe of his cowboy boot, and kicked them towards me. "Think fast. Maybe we'll have to drive by your school."

"What for?" Mom asked as I snatched the keys and ran into the bathroom to change into my smock top.

Not long after my birthday, when my brother had returned to work, I was in the bathtub soaking in Strawberry Fields Bath Foam. With the help of many bobby pins and my vanity mirror, I had pulled my shag haircut on top of my head. The bathroom window was wide open to vent my cigarette smoke. Having just mastered French inhaling, I admired my skill in the reflection on the faucet. Take a drag, extend the lower lip, inhale through the nose. A stream of smoke entered each nostril. I couldn't wait to show Cindy.

When the doorbell rang, I extinguished my cigarette in the bathwater. Sitting absolutely still in the pink-tinged bubbles, I listened to Mom crossing the slate to answer the door. I heard men's voices, unusual at our house, especially at night, especially with Tom back at the rig. I couldn't distinguish their words but I could tell there were two men talking to my Mom. I hopped out of the tub, flushed the cigarette butt down the toilet, and wrapped a towel around myself. Checking the mirror, I decided my hair looked sophisticated so I left it pinned on top of my head. I thoroughly brushed my teeth to cover my cigarette breath.

My Mom was alone, standing in the kitchen with her arms crossed, her hands grasping her forearms.

"Your brother's been killed, Sweetie," she said.

"Who killed him?" I asked, tightening the towel around my body.

"An accident at the rig."

"So no one really 'killed' him." I yanked at the towel to keep it from sliding down my narrow chest.

"The body will be here tomorrow." Mom filled the kettle with water.

"Tom's body. Not 'the' body. Tom's body." I knew I was being unfair, but I couldn't stop.

Mom plugged in the kettle and rubbed the sailboat on her neck. "I'll have to plan a funeral."

"Tom's funeral," I said, shaking my fists and letting the towel slide off my body. Not 'a funeral.'"

Mom looked vacantly at me, asked, "Tea?"

The next day, Cindy flopped onto our couch, still wiping away tears. She pulled the box of Kleenex onto her stomach. "Oh my God, this is so awful. At least you have the stuffed mouse."

"I'm going to pitch it."

"Oh no, Diane, my God, you can't do that."

"That's what I'm going to do."

"Don't throw it out. It means too much. I'll take it."

"Be my guest."

"Fine. I will." Sniffling and snuffling, Cindy maneuvered the giant mouse out our front door and carried it home to her bedroom, where she impaled it on her bedpost.

My Mom wrote a short obituary for the newspaper and included a goofy-looking picture of my brother in Grade 10. When the obituary appeared in the newspaper, she read it carefully. Finding no errors, she scrunched the newspaper into two balls and took them to the gym bag at the front door. The gym bag, delivered by the funeral home, contained the clothes Tom had been wearing on the rig when the pipe slipped. Mom unzipped the bag and pulled out my brother's snakeskin shit-kickers. She sat on the bottom step of the stairway, stuffing the newspaper deep into the boots.

"To keep the shape," she said, as she carried the boots up to Tom's bedroom. Hours passed before I heard Mom close Tom's closet and walk down the hall to her own room.

In the many years that have passed since my big brother's death, I have never missed that stuffed mouse. And last month, while cleaning out my Mom's house, I did not hesitate before dropping Tom's flaking cowboy boots into the garbage. My son, who was supposed to be helping me pack things up, retrieved the boots and tried them on. He clomped around the house for almost an hour before declaring that the boots stunk like pizza farts. And that's when my stomach tensed up like it used to when I was a kid. Because, even though I see my son without shoes all the time, when he kicked off those shit-kickers, I was taken aback by the tender whiteness of his feet.

BASIC OBEDIENCE

By the time he retired from teaching math and physics at Campbell Heights Senior High School, Simon had been heckled by obnoxious students, threatened by a father whose child's mark had dropped from 90 to 88 percent, stalked by a gang member who flunked Math 14, and tackled by a drunk student while chaperoning a school dance. On the home front, after Simon's wife died from a cancer that took her voice before it stopped her life, he had raised their daughter Alicia mostly on his own, arranging after-school care and play dates, and carpooling and working casino nights for Alicia's hoity-toity gymnastics club. None of this prepared him for the stress of dog classes.

Simon doesn't even own a dog. Cooper, his dog "partner," belongs to Alicia. Technically, Cooper also belongs to Alicia's boyfriend, Justin. Alicia and Justin got the dog the day they moved in together, and split the cost—which amounted to a donation to the SPCA to cover the cost of neutering. Alicia and Justin split the cost of everything precisely down the middle: the rent, the groceries, every tank of gas, every latte and apple. Simon figures that if Justin bought a pack of gum and gave Alicia a piece, he would charge her for it. Alicia would hand over the dime without a hint of complaint. Justin and Alicia make about the same amount of money, so Simon knows the cost-splitting shouldn't irritate him. But it does.

Simon and Cooper are on their way to dog class. The Dog Corral is a forty-five-minute drive from Simon's house, but conveniently close to Alicia and Justin's condo. Alicia had intended to take Cooper to the classes herself. Then her shift work as a nurse interfered and Justin always said he had to meet clients at night for his insurance sales job, so Simon was recruited. "Please, Dad? Our place would be so much more peaceful if Cooper had proper training. You'd be good for him." What was a dad to do with a request like that, combined with the stressed tremor in Alicia's voice? Suggest they never should have got Cooper in the first place? No, that was not possible knowing how much Alicia loved that dog.

Simon parks his car behind the Dog Corral, where spring grass has started to grow on the median. Cooper whines. Simon gathers up the leash and the bag of dog treats and opens the back door, clipping the leash on Cooper's collar. They walk back and forth in the parking lot, Simon hoping that Cooper will have a pee and a crap before class.

Cooper pees on the median. He tries to crap, but without success. Simon can hear the other dogs barking at the front of the building. Cooper strains a few more times, until Simon, checking his watch and seeing they are late, decides to leave the crap to fate. They walk around the building to the front door of the Dog Corral, not on a loose lead, like they are supposed to, but with Cooper lunging ahead. The trainer, a sporty and chipper woman in her fifties, holds the door open, says, "Who's walking who?"

"We get the general idea," Simon says.

Inside the Dog Corral, several dogs and owners are already heeling around the room, following the trainer's orders. "Fast. Slow. Right about-turn. Left about-turn." Cooper stalls in confusion. Simon tries to encourage him with treats and the high-pitched happy-chat the trainer suggests. Cooper switches gears and darts sideways, then barks and jumps up on Simon. Finally, Simon sits on one of the chairs set up against the wall. He closes a treat in his fist, and lets Cooper lick his knuckles. They can kill a lot of time this way.

One Golden Retriever, two Labs, a Bichon, a Boston Terrier, one annoying cattle dog that does everything right, and two medium-sized, pointy-nosed black dogs that look quite a bit like Cooper. Until recently, Simon has never noticed that Cooper and his look-alikes seem to be the genetic default for mutts. Simon has never owned a dog, but he fancies himself a beagle man. He read a story once about a retired professor who went for long walks on the moors every day—a scone in his pocket and a beagle at his side. Once Alicia and Justin have more time to take care of Cooper, Simon will get a beagle and name it Pythagoras. No he won't. He wants more time to golf, not more time at the Dog Corral.

Now the trainer, using her what-a-good-dog voice, announces that they are going to work on their long sit-stays. Simon takes Cooper into the circle of dogs, gives Cooper the sit signal by putting his right hand to his own shoulder, and throws in what he imagines is a stern look. Cooper sits for a few seconds, whines, wriggles, then walks toward Simon. Simon gives the signal again. Cooper manages a low squat.

"Is Cooper's bum okay?" the trainer asks.

Simon senses the eyes of all the owners and dogs shifting in his direction. He feels as if the class is looking at his bum, not Cooper's.

"Superb," Simon says, patting his own shoulder vigorously so as to emphasize to Cooper that a true sit requires a dog's back end on the floor.

"At least he keeps eye contact," the trainer says.

Cooper sits for a few more seconds and the trainer moves on to the Boston Terrier.

All the other dogs sit obediently, smug as their owners. It is so true, Simon thinks, that people resemble their dogs. Not in the direct way that they show on TV. But in a feeling, a *je ne sais quoi*, as the folks in the French department at Campbell Heights would say. The cattle dog's owner, for instance, is a woman with matching shoes, belt, and treat bag, and a tense watchfulness about her, even though her dog has never broken a sit or stay. That dog will probably take down an escaped convict some day, but it still won't be enough to make the owner satisfied or relaxed.

Cooper has eyes like Alicia's. They are not the exact same shape or colour—after all, Cooper is a dog—but they emit the same worrisome combination of eagerness and vulnerability. No convicts will be hauled to the ground by these two. Cooper and Alicia think everyone is good.

"One minute to go," the trainer calls.

Cooper momentarily settles his butt on the floor and then picks it up again, hovering in a strange, thigh-bursting position. This particular weirdness about sitting is new, but Cooper's inability to sit for more than two seconds is perennial. He is the only dog in the class that has not mastered the sit-stay. In a way, Simon admires this imperviousness to training. As a teacher, he was always drawn to the kids who questioned, the ones who didn't follow the pack. But if he is going to be of any help to Alicia, some results with Cooper are necessary. He walks Cooper over to the water bowl and waits until the sit exercise is over.

"Release your dogs," the trainer says.

Cooper's ears perk up and he happily prances back to their spot in the room as though he has accomplished as much as the other dogs. Simon pats Cooper. Says "Good dog" like everyone else.

Next it's the down-stay with distraction—Cooper's specialty, and the high point in every class. Simon puts his arm in the air and Cooper plops down. Cooper stares right at Simon throughout the exercise, even though the trainer is bouncing tennis balls and rolling baby strollers; even though the Bichon, who seemed to be such a sweetie in the sit-stay, suddenly goes berserk on the Golden Retriever. This moves the Bichon and its shamed owner to the bottom of the class, thus bumping Simon and Cooper up a notch.

While Cooper relaxes into his down-stay, Simon thinks about how the front end of the dog reminds him of Alicia, and the back end reminds him of Justin. Not that Simon has any concrete reason to think that Justin is an ass. Justin is hard-working, smart, good-looking. Always respectful to Simon. Alicia was so thrilled with Justin that she moved in with him three months after they met. They got Cooper before Alicia finished unpacking. Alicia had always wanted a dog, but when she was growing up Simon had felt they didn't have the time to properly take care of a dog. Simon admits that he is jealous that Justin fulfilled this wish of Alicia's. And he admits that he misses Alicia and wants to blame the void on Justin. But there is something else, too. Justin's perfectness. There was an English teacher at Campbell Heights who showed up perfect every day. She always got her marks in on time, never got sarcastic, never raised her voice or cried. One day, she came to school in her usual tailored blouse and skirt and pantyhose, but wearing pink terry-towel slippers. She taught her morning classes, and then walked in her slippers down the block to the medi-centre, where she had a complete breakdown.

"Release your dogs," the trainer says to the class. She claps her hands, then she speaks directly to Simon and Cooper. "Wow. What a look. You are that dog's hero."

The next day, Simon drives over to Alicia and Justin's place. He lets himself in. Cooper jumps on him, overjoyed, undisciplined. Simon raises his arm, Cooper drops to a down-stay, tail wagging, until Simon releases him. Simon finds a pen and a scrap of paper in the kitchen, writes a note for Alicia, then drives Cooper to the vet.

The vet pokes and prods Cooper, says, "He's had some trauma back there. Has he been out of your sight at any time? Got a rough neighbour who might've given him the boot?"

"He's not my dog," Simon says. "I just take him to school."

"You know the owners?"

"Not really well."

"Let's take an x-ray to be sure."

Two hundred dollars later, Simon drives Cooper back to Justin and Alicia's condo. The x-ray didn't show anything definitive. Simon opens the door to the condo and lets Cooper in. He fills Cooper's dish with fresh water. Alicia comes into the kitchen.

"Hi dad."

"Hi Al, just dropping off Cooper."

Alicia looks terrible. Puffy-eyed and pale. She's still in her purple nursing scrubs, but the shirt with the big pockets at her hips and the sprinkling of tiny happy faces doesn't mask the exhausted raggedness about her. Simon hopes her appearance is just due to a long shift at the hospital.

"Thanks for taking him to the vet. I thought maybe something was wrong when I walked him yesterday."

"The vet couldn't find anything."

"That's good."

Alicia crouches on the floor, nose-to-nose with Cooper. She kisses his forehead. Cooper steps into her and rests his head on her shoulder, pushing her hair back from her face. Simon sees that Alicia's earlobe is cut and swollen.

"What happened to your ear?" Simon asks. "I should have taken you to the doctor instead of taking doofus here to the vet."

Alicia pulls the hair back over her ear. "I'll get it checked at the hospital next shift. Caught my hoop earring on the bedpost. What did the vet cost?"

"My treat."

"At least let me make you some coffee."

"Not a chance. You get some sleep, Alicia."

"I'm going to wait up and make dinner for Justin."

"He can make his own dinner."

"I know. He's a terrific cook. I just feel like doing it."

Simon reaches into the back pocket of his jeans, pulls out his leather wallet, and lays a stack of bills on the counter. "Phone for pizza, eat it, and go to bed."

"Aw, Dad, we don't need your money. We've got good jobs."

"Just take it," Simon says, putting his wallet back in his jeans. "Order enough pizza for the rest of the week. And get your ear checked."

"Justin doesn't like pizza," Alicia says.

Simon bends, gives Cooper a gentle pat on the ribs. When he looks up, Alicia is slipping the money into the front pocket of her scrubs. He pats Cooper again, says, "Okay then, I've got to get home. Let me know what they say about your ear."

On the way home, Simon wonders about getting a hoop earring caught on a bedpost. Can that happen? Maybe. But Alicia gave the explanation to Cooper rather than him, a classic avoidance technique. Years of teaching have made Simon pretty good at identifying the words and mannerisms of liars.

The morning of the next dog class, Simon's friend Gerry calls.

"Simon, let the season begin. I've got a four o'clock tee time."

"I don't know, Gerry, I feel like I should go to dog classes."

"That dog's more hassle than a grandchild."

"It's just that I've been taking him and now, even though Justin can take him tonight, I feel like I'm letting the dog down."

"Justin is a big boy. He can handle the dog."

"I guess you're right."

"Four o'clock."

Simon hangs up the phone. He vacuums, forwards email jokes to other retired teachers. He knows the jokes aren't funny and that he is procrastinating. Then he gets out his clubs and golf shoes from the basement. Sure, Justin can take the dog. It's his dog. There won't be any last-minute requests for Simon to be at dog training since Justin is on an investment course and finishing early every day. Justin told Simon that insurance isn't simple anymore; it's about sliding the life insurance policy in with other products.

Gerry is on the tee box, swinging his club like he's at home plate. Since Gerry was a baseball umpire before retirement, he never learned how to golf properly; he always worked through the golf season.

"You sick or somethin'?" Gerry asks Simon.

"Thinking about the dog, I guess."

Gerry hits his drive down the fairway, not far, not straight. "You're up, dog-boy," he says.

Simon's tee shot and approach shots turn out better than he feels. His intuition about the strength of the wind is smack on, each shot landing on the intended mark. At the green, Gerry starts humming the old Hockey Night in Canada theme song like he always does, and pulls out his putter. He makes a big show of reading the green, then sinks the ball.

"Simon," Gerry says as he bends to retrieve the ball. "Putt, then get the hell out of here. You're a mope. Go to dog class. I'll catch up to the threesome ahead of us."

Simon drives to the Dog Corral. He parks and peaks in the window. Cooper is doing a long down. Rather than staring at Justin, Cooper's head is bowed, eyes cast at the floor.

Simon gets back in his car and waits until the class is over. When he sees Justin and Cooper leaving the Dog Corral, he gets out to meet them. Justin is dressed in tailored slacks and a button-up shirt and jacket, which is what he wears most of the time, but his attire still makes Simon think of parent-teacher interview nights at the school, and he steels himself accordingly.

"Hi there, Simon, what's up?" Justin asks.

Before Simon can respond, Cooper goes all nutty and jumps on him. Justin jerks the leash to pull Cooper off, then swings open the hatchback door to his car. He grabs Cooper around the waist and tosses him in. Simon knows this is not the time to comment on the roughness. His years of dealing with difficult students at Campbell Heights taught him that confrontation only works when you've got nothing to lose.

"Just getting some of those lamb dog treats that they sell at the desk here," Simon says once the hatchback is closed. "You and Cooper heading home?"

"Picking up Alicia from work."

"Something the matter with her car?"

"I drove her in today. I've got the time, now. We're thinking of selling her car."

Simon nods.

Justin gets in his car, starts the engine. Then he rolls down the window. "Thanks for taking Coop to the vet the other day," Justin says.

"Anytime," Simon says. "You know, the vet thought Cooper might have been kicked."

Justin laughs, says, "What did he charge for that diagnosis?"

"Not much," Simon says. "Seemed like a deal to me."

"Well, thanks again," Justin says, as he rolls up the

window.

Simon watches the back of the car as Justin drives out of the parking lot. Cooper is in the hatch, his ears laid flat against his head, his dark eyes locked onto Simon.

When Simon can no longer see Cooper, he turns and walks into the Dog Corral. He will enroll Cooper in the next set of classes: Advanced and Games. After that, he and Cooper will be eligible for Agility. Maybe even Flyball. Whatever it takes, for however long it takes, for Alicia's sake.

EULOGY FOR THE FEMINIST MOVEMENT

I paid attention to my socks this morning. The first pair I put on, red wool shin-highs with fading reindeer and threadbare soles, are my favourites. They are like me and my saggy old feminist friends—comfortable, functional, and clearly approaching our expiry date. Then I revised my sock decision since, as a woman going to an OB/GYN appointment, an appointment where my socks will be prominent, although not front and centre, threadbare won't do. And considering Christmas is months away, reindeer won't do. After rummaging around in my drawer, through executive trouser socks and sturdy hikers, I decided on short tennis socks that speak of physical fitness, although they have never been used for that purpose.

The nurses always say, "Take everything off from the waist down, but you can leave your socks on." I suppose it's just a roundabout way of saying, "Uncover your pooty." There may very well be women who put their bare feet in the stirrups. But until doctors think to update their 18th-century stirrups with something else—say, a carpeted footrest—I will be a sock woman.

As it turns out, when I get to the appointment, Dr. Duescher's nurse tells me the doctor will come talk to me first, then I will uncover my pooty. The nurse offers to stay in the room during the examination. This is a new option for me; I have never gone to a male doctor before. Surely there's only room for one medical professional to be working down there. I say no thanks.

In my younger days, I made a special point of only going to female doctors. They were paid less, were respected less, and the men sure weren't going to them. Then, as time passed, I went to female doctors out of habit. But here I am, referred to Dr. Duescher, the senior specialist at the Centre for Women's Health, for a biopsy. He wears a navy cardigan and a humble-pie smile. Mr. Rogers as an OB/GYN.

We shake hands. He looks at my file.

"I see you work," he says.

This is obviously a lame attempt at pre-stirrup conversation. But at least it's an attempt, so I give him a break.

"I teach women's studies," I say, which is a bit of a lie. I retired last year when the department shut down the women's studies program. There's still a course, one course—"History of Women and Activism"—but there's no degree program anymore due to lack of enrollment.

It seems Dr. Duescher isn't interested in where I work or what I teach because, instead of inquiring further, he says, "Okey-doke, let's have a look at you. I'll be back in a few minutes. Get yourself ready. Don't be cluttering your head with worry about this."

I'm not worried; I'm way over that. My mother and aunt died of cervical cancer. I have the same symptoms. It was bound to come down the tubes, so to speak. The whole point of this visit, to me, is a rubber stamp that says "uterine cancer."

Jeans and underwear off. Given the nature of the appointment, I didn't spend as much time considering my underwear as I did my socks. I tuck my greying, stretched-out jockeys under my jeans on the chair. Then I get on the examination table, sit my bare ass on the white paper sheet and cover myself from the waist down with the blue cloth sheet. The cloth sheet is a definite upgrade from the paper sheet at my regular doctor's.

There's a soft knock at the door, followed by Duescher coming back into the room.

"You can lie down," he says. "Slip your feet in the stirrups."

I lie down, adjust the cloth sheet over my knees to create the peculiar open-door tent that doctors like to work under. The window at the end of the bed is wide open, blowing fresh air up my pooty, not in a bad way at all. My regular doctor's office doesn't have any windows. This warm

September breeze, I must say, is a treat.

"Scoot down," Duescher says as he gathers his instruments together and walks to the end of the bed.

I scoot.

"Little more scoot," he says.

I scoot, thinking it was nicer when Dr. Duescher wasn't blocking the breeze.

"Bit more, please," he says.

I feel satisfied with my white socks. There would have been something crass about having my big old toes on either side of this man's head.

I have a fairly clear mental image of what he's looking at down there. In the '70s, I went to several of those parties where we all brought a hand mirror, dropped our pants and bikini underwear, got in a squat and had a good look at ourselves. Back then it never occurred to me to evaluate if everything looked "right." But that's an issue now. One of my former students sent me a note to say that my class had empowered her to get a vagina job. To make everything more even and rose-buddish, she said. I'm not sure how she got that sort of empowerment from my teachings. Yes, it was time to retire.

Speculum will be first, I assume. Not that I can see one. But, before I feel anything, Dr. Duescher's head pops up from under my tent.

"Seen the stock market today?" he says.

"The what?"

"The stock market. It's jumping."

Duescher keeps looking at me, so I fumble for a

response. I don't think he's senile—probably just trying to make conversation, make me relax.

"I'm not a player," I say.

He goes back under the sheet. Ah, there's the speculum. Inserted. Another archaic tool.

Duescher's head pops up again.

"You could be a player," he says. "It's not hard. I know some women who do really well in it."

What to say to that? I raise my head. He seems, again, to require a response before he goes back to work.

"I know some women who have lost a lot of money," I say.

"Well now, let's not be negative about the whole stock market based on a few bad experiences."

Back under the sheet. Good, I'm thinking, get in there. Do your job, man. And as though he's heard me, he starts snooping around, inspecting my love canal for hedge funds, pork bellies, cancer—that sort of thing.

In my early twenties, when feminism was both stylish and politically correct, my friends and I spent a lot of time discussing the plight of women and, more frequently, the nomenclature for women's genitalia. Men had so many names for their genitals—friendly, racy, courageous, superhuman names. Everything from Admiral Dong to General Zibi. In the interest of equality, we felt we needed just as many names, preferably something more inspired than the few existing animal references. I can't remember all the suggestions, although I do recall liking Atlantis and the Zen Palace. My boyfriend at the time, a slightly anemic biology major, once joined in the discussion and suggested the Bearded Clam.

The clattering at the end of the table suggests Dr. Duescher is switching utensils. More metal, no doubt. Those little forceps?

One of my formerly-feminist friends had her children late in life. I was at her house the other day and I heard her refer to her daughter's pooty as a "front bum." Now there's a kid who is going to be messed up. She won't know her ass from a hole in the ground, or her back ass from her front bum.

My thoughts are interrupted by a fire alarm ringing on another floor. Duescher probably can't hear it, ensconced as he is between my thighs under the blue sheet. I'm not too concerned about Duescher or the fire alarm. But then, with an ear-splitting jolt, the alarm starts ringing on this floor. It feels like the bell is right outside the door of my examination room. I hate the idea of going down in flames.

Duescher must hear it now, yet he stays under the sheet. Is he deaf? He's putting more metal up my front bum. Whatever it is that will perform the cervical punch? Maybe that was the forceps. I've lost track. With the alarm blaring, I pride myself on the fact that I don't clench. Anything.

I wait a moment, then prop myself up on my elbows. I don't want firefighters rushing in here while I'm in the stirrups. "Hello?" I shout between my knees.

"There we go," Duescher says loudly as he comes out from under the blue sheet. He plops a small amount of fibrousy red stuff, like red algae, combined with blood from my ongoing periods, in a jar and walks over to the sink. He pours tap water into the jar and snaps on a lid.

"Just about done," he says. "But first I better go see what all the noise is about." He leaves the room with the jar.

I sit all the way up, dangling my legs between the stirrups. From this position I can look out the window and see a fire truck parked on the lawn. A second fire truck pulls up, lights flashing. I hop off the bed, pull on my underwear, jeans, shoes. I open the door. The hall is lit by floor lights—the regular overhead lights are off. The exit sign at the end of the hall is glowing.

Dr. Duescher is nowhere to be seen. Semi-dressed women peek out of doors along the corridor. One woman walks down the hall wearing a paper gown, a short jacket on top, a big purse slung over her shoulder, her back bum hanging out. The woman directly across the hall from me is hugely pregnant, dressed in a white tailored shirt and bare from the waist down except for the blue sheet wrapped around her waist. Business on the top, gyno on the bottom.

"What should we do?" the pregnant woman mouths. Maybe she says it out loud.

"I'm going," I point to the emergency exit.

She points to her sheet, motions that she's going to put clothes on her bottom half.

I grab my purse from the chair in the examination room and head toward the exit sign.

The stairwell is full of women. Employees, nurses, doctors, many in ponytails and pink Crocs. Patients ranging from solid teenage girls to sparrowy grandmas—all abandoning the Centre for Women's Health. There are no flames, no smoke, and yet we hurry. Clearly no one wants to be left inside.

Once on the front lawn, I wait, making sure that I see the pregnant woman from my corridor come out. Women continue to pour from the doors. Some have even started to run. Finally, amidst the crowd, I see the pregnant woman. She's skirted and panty-hosed and ready for work. I try to catch her eye but she is hustling away from the building.

Over in the centre of the lawn, I see Dr. Duescher talking with half a dozen men. Are they all doctors? Could be. I know the stats—I used to teach them. If there were one hundred men standing there, only 6.78 percent of them might be nurses. Some are young but one—a tanned, wiry man—is even older than Duescher and seems to hold rank. He's telling a joke or a funny story and making a lusty big-boob motion with his hands. The men break out in hearty laughter. I wonder if Duescher dropped my biopsy jar at the lab before he left the building.

I decide I'm done for the day and head for my car. Just like Duescher said, no need to clutter my head with worry about the biopsy. But after thirty years of devoting myself to women's studies, thirty years of active involvement in the women's movement (the second wave, that is, which will likely be renamed the final wave), still plenty to worry about.

Three days later (that's how it goes in cases like mine) I'm back at the Centre for Women's Health for the biopsy result. I'm fully clothed, sitting in the vinyl-covered chair, my feet flat on the floor. I'm wearing my reindeer socks.

"Okay, let's see what we've got here," Dr. Duescher says, scanning his chart.

He sits down, lifts a page, looks at the page underneath.

"I see you work," he says.

"I'm the one who was under examination when the fire alarm went off."

"Alarms are always going off in here. It's an old system. I'm used to it. We all are."

"I'll never be used to it," I say.

Duescher sets the clipboard beside the sink, earnestly clasps his hands together. "Honey," he says, "have you seen the stock market today?"

THANKSGIVING

From my chair on the porch, I can see the bottom half of Bob Stead. He's in his fir trees, trimming off dead branches, tidying nature. Bob calls it fire-smarting; I call it unnecessary. Bob begins to descend the ladder with a branch in one hand, and Barclay, my German Shepherd who is waiting at the bottom of the ladder, gets excited. Bob shakes the branch at Barclay. Barclay bites one leg of the ladder, tugs. Bob lunges at the tree for balance.

I'm down my porch stairs by then. Yelling at Barclay. I grab a handful of skin and bristling hair from the back of Barclay's neck. He's on his hind legs, barking.

"Throw the branch," I shout. "Throw it."

Bob tosses the branch towards his deer feeder. Barclay jumps out of my grip, dives on the branch. Tail wagging, branch held high, he prances past the deer feeder, up the hill. I steady the ladder. Bob hurries down.

"Control your dog," he says, flapping his work glove in my face.

In town, later that afternoon, at the A&G grocery, I spot Bob's wife Cheryl in the root vegetable section.

"Hello Stanley," she says, smiling a bit, folding her hands on her pregnant belly. "All ready for Thanksgiving?"

"I suppose. You doing a big bird?"

"Oh yes, we always do. It's in the oven. You off to friends?"

"No."

Cheryl picks up a potato, rolls it in her hand. "Well, of course you're welcome at our place. I don't think Bob would mind, really. I could reset the table, put you beside my mother, across from Jonathan."

"What time?" I ask as she untwists her plastic bag, drops the extra potato on top of four already there, and pushes her cart towards the pumpkins.

When my mother was alive she always made me put on a button-front shirt for turkey dinners. For her sake, I wear one of the green shirts I used to wear when I drove to work in the city. The collar cinches around my neck, the buttons at my chest are strained. That's one good thing about being laid off from the water treatment plant. No more uncomfortable clothes.

Bob and Cheryl's dining room smells of warm turkey and pine walls. There's a sliding door at one end that opens onto their new cedar deck and groomed lawn. The table is big, harvest style. Four baby pumpkins surround a large red candle centrepiece. Every place has a turkey napkin and a turkey plate.

I sit beside the grandmother. She's on a weekend pass. Her balding head shakes no non-stop. The other three seats are empty. Bob stands at the pine sideboard, working the cork out of a bottle of wine. Bob is a surgeon in the city. He's the kind of guy who wears pleated pants on the weekend. The kind of guy who vacuums his garage and volunteers every year for the community water co-op. I hear Cheryl running the tap in the kitchen. Bleeps and snippets of electronic songs arise from downstairs. Jonathan must be playing computer games. He's a good kid. Only been caught shoplifting once (or so I heard at the A&G). Nothing serious, just candy. Cheryl claims that Jonathan's mathematically gifted. He plays one of those hand-held computer games while he walks home from the school bus stop. I watch from my porch, expect him to stumble, but he never does. Maybe he is gifted.

Cheryl rushes into the room and sets a bowl of cranberry sauce on the table. She's wearing pressed pants and a leaf-print maternity blouse. Her belly protrudes like a gourd from her thin body. On her way back to the kitchen, she stops at the sliding door.

"Bob." She taps the toe of her penny loafer at a spot on the floor in front of her.

"I'll speak to him again," Bob says.

"He's got to learn. Just look at the dirt he's tracked in."

Bob leaves the room, thumps downstairs, stops the electronic sounds. The grandmother puts her shaky hand on my arm and asks for a taste of wine. Noticing that she doesn't have a wineglass at her place, I fill my own and offer it to her.

"Might help my memory," the grandmother says.

"Mine too," I say, pouring wine into my water glass.

Jonathan sulks into the dining room. The bottoms of his pantlegs drag across the hardwood. His sweatshirt is huge, big enough to fit me. It's the same outfit his skateboard buddies wear at the A&G parking lot. Nice for him to have so many friends. I nod hello. He scowls, slouches into the seat across from me. I like Jonathan.

"A touch more, if you don't mind," the grandmother says. I steady her glass on the table and pour. Jonathan brightens.

"Mom," he yells into the kitchen, "Stanley's giving grandma wine."

Cheryl appears at the door to the dining room, pauses, inhales. "It's Mr. Davis to you," she says to Jonathan while she scoops the wineglass out of her mother's hand.

When Bob sets the huge, caramel-coloured turkey in front of him, the table looks like a picture from a magazine. Bob twists the first drumstick from the turkey. Juice drips from the joint. I take in the deep hot smell.

"Dad," Jonathan asks as we begin passing vegetables, "can I eat in front of the TV?"

Bob rips open the breast skin with the tip of the carving knife.

"Daaaad," Jonathan pleads.

"This is Thanksgiving," says Bob. "You'll appreciate the memories when you're older."

"Mom?"

Cheryl shoves a casserole dish at him. "It's tradition. Would you like some cauliflower in low-fat cheese sauce?"

Jonathan picks up the serving spoon, mutters, "Who cares." I slide the mashed potatoes towards the grandmother. She waves them off, saying, "Just fiddleheads for me."

"There are no fiddleheads." Cheryl snaps her turkey napkin and drapes it over her belly. "You're in Alberta."

"Don't we usually have turnips at Thanksgiving?" Bob asks.

"No, potatoes. We always have potatoes," Cheryl says.

"I'm sure we had turnips last year." Bob picks up his knife and fork. "We should write these things down in a notebook."

"I don't need to write it down," Cheryl glares at Bob. Then Bob says he'll have some potatoes. Cheryl turns to me, smiling. "Now Stanley, I'm sure this won't stand up at all to your mother's Thanksgiving dinners."

I'm glad to be a part of the conversation, so I say, "My mother's turkey was always drier than a pretzel fart. Stuffing like freeze-dried sewage."

Cheryl looks across the table at Bob.

"And mother's gravy always made me think of diarrhea," I add, "or vomit."

"Nice," Jonathan says.

"I know you're not supposed to say that sort of thing about your mother, especially if she's dead, but I call 'em as I see 'em."

Cheryl looks at her plate. Bob wipes his mouth.

"It's Harvard beets and black licorice that give me the runs," the grandmother says. I like the grandmother.

Through the sliding door, past the deck, smack in the middle of Bob's neat lawn, a loosely woven hammock of hay hangs inside a small wooden shelter. Bob's dream is to have deer browsing in his backyard. He'd especially like them there when his city friends come out for dinner.

"Much luck with the deer feeder?" I ask while I reach across Cheryl for carrots even though they don't look buttered.

"Not one," Jonathan interjects. "Zippo."

"They're all over my place," I say. "Barclay's got more deer than he knows how to chase." Funny that the deer don't go for Bob's lawn. He takes good care of it—he's always aerating or fertilizing or watering or pumping clover kill on it. At my place the deer eat the quack grass, the clover, even the thistles that grow on the gravel pile. Like I keep telling Bob when he asks, I'm going to spread that gravel someday and make a pen for Barclay.

It's dusk by the time I scrape up my second helping. Everyone else is still picking at their first. I usually don't notice vegetables, always ate my mother's chilled Brussels sprouts and marshmallow turnips without complaint, but Cheryl's vegetables are different. The carrots are sweet and seasoned with green flecks, and the potatoes soak up buckets of the smooth gravy. I even take more low-fat cauliflower. There's lots of food, maybe because the grandmother only eats cranberry sauce. Red rivulets form in the lines under her lips. I take a breather, lean back from the table and look out the sliding door. Three mule deer file down the hill and eye the feeder.

"Got yourself some deer." I wave my fork towards the sliding door.

Bob runs for his camera. Aware of Bob's motion, the deer stop, ears wide, tails tucked under, and stare through the window at us. Cheryl crouches beside the grandmother, points, repeats, "Deer, Mom. Outside. Deer." She pats the grandmother's hand and goes to the window to stand beside Jonathan, presses her palms into the small of her back, pushes her belly towards the glass. The grandmother nudges me. I fill her water glass with wine. "Too bad about the fiddleheads," I say.

Bob returns with his camera, slowly opens the sliding door, pushes the big lens outside. A black-tipped tail quivers, rises. The *tharump* of padded feet sounds from the side of the house, louder and louder until Barclay careens around the corner. The deer spring up the hill. Barclay charges after them, a frayed metre of rope dragging from his neck.

"Look at them go!" Jonathan cries. "Yeesss!"

Bob slides the door closed, flips the lock.

"Barclay never did like being tied up," I say as Bob sits heavily in his seat. "Maybe I should get that pen built."

Cheryl takes the gravy boat and potatoes into the

kitchen.

"Did you see that Dad? Did you?" Jonathan pokes his fork into the pool of liquid wax surrounding the red candle.

"Stop that," Bob says sharply.

"My mother made the best chow-chow relish in Moncton," says the grandmother.

I pour her some more wine. She wipes under her eyes with her turkey napkin. Jonathan stabs a baby pumpkin with his fork.

"Mom," he yells into the kitchen, "she's crying." Cheryl hurries into the dining room.

"Pie, everyone?" she asks, discreetly laying a stack of tissue on the grandmother's lap.

Mom and I bought our house twenty years ago, when she retired. We got a good deal because the original owners divorced and sold before the house was finished. Mom and I finished the drywalling and put on the porch. We used that porch almost every day. This time of year there'd be owls in the woodpile, squirrels in the empty bird feeder, chickadees and siskins in the firs, and deer. Right up to her last day, Mom could identify any critter or plant within a half-mile of the house. She thought it took me a long time to learn all the names in nature. But I pretended not to know things just so we could keep talking.

Jonathan's chair scrapes when he pushes away from the table. As he turns to look at the damage he's done to the hardwood floor, something outside seems to catch his eye. He stands, presses his face against the glass door.

"Dad, I think Barclay's out there again."

Bob gets up, joins Jonathan at the sliding door, and squints through the glass into the dark. "Hunched, maybe a porcupine or raccoon."

"Why don't you go outside and get a good look?" I suggest from my chair.

"Dad, I think it's Barclay."

Bob reaches for the switch beside the door and flicks on the outside lights. Barclay, caught in the light beam on the lawn, perks his ears. His tail, stiff and curved like a hockey stick, jerks up and down while he pumps a dump onto the grass. He stops, peeks behind him, kicks back a little dirt, and trots onto the deck.

"He wants in," Jonathan says, grabbing the handle of the sliding door.

Bob takes a deep breath and holds it before he says, "I don't think Barclay's an indoor dog."

"Sure he is," I say.

"Dad?"

Bob goes to the sideboard, pours a tumbler of Scotch. I empty the last of the second bottle of wine into my glass.

"I don't care," Bob says to the ceiling. "Take him to the basement." Before Jonathan scuffs out of the dining room, one hand on the piece of rope dangling from Barclay's neck, the other hand gently patting Barclay on the head, Bob adds, "And get some pants that fit."

Cheryl brings in a special pot of tea for the grandmother and pours coffee for me and Bob.

"What are you hoping for?" I ask, pointing at her belly.

"Oh, a girl would be nice. You know, one boy, one girl. That would be perfect."

The grandmother farts. A real long *pu-pu-pu-pu-pup*. Cheryl wipes vigorously at the glass on the sliding door with her turkey napkin. She complains about fingerprints.

While Bob and Cheryl move dishes to the kitchen, I pour myself a little Grand Marnier from the sideboard and think of how, when I was a kid, Mom and I would throw the football around on Thanksgiving. She was a big woman and could catch and pass as good as anyone. She'd have me running patterns right through dusk and, sometimes, depending on the brightness of the sky, into the night. Mom played in a dress—a housedress, she called it—with a pair of my sweatpants pulled up underneath. She always licked her fingertips before placing them across the laces on the ball.

"Say, Bob," I call into the kitchen, "you play football?"

"No," Bob yells back, as though he is scolding a dog.

"Bob!" Cheryl says. The kitchen tap is turned on.

The grandmother rattles her teacup in the saucer. I top her up with Grand Marnier. The outside lights are still on. I watch the deer, the same three females as before, approach the feeder, tentatively pulling some hay from the hammock. Dishes clatter in the kitchen. Bob enters the dining room, flicks off the outside light, grabs the Grand Marnier from in front of me and puts it on the sideboard.

"Got some deer out there again," I tell him.

"I'll take that coffee mug for you." Bob clears my place.

My mother played football with me right up to her final Thanksgiving. She could still throw a spiral over the gravel pile, but by then, I didn't very often return her throws. I ran it back. She kept our football pumped up tighter than a rock and I was afraid I'd break her hands if I fired the ball into her. Not that her hands were fragile, or even small.

Cheryl helps the grandmother up from the table.

"Maples," the grandmother says to me, still holding a tissue to her eyes, "you can't imagine the Moncton maples this time of year."

"Mom's off to bed," Cheryl says as she steers the grandmother towards the door.

"Goodnight," I say.

"Goodnight, sweet prince," the grandmother calls happily over her shoulder.

Bob shrugs, pours only himself a drink, even though I push my glass towards him, and tells me, like he always does, that he's so sorry, really sorry, about how close he built to my house. I never reply because, as my mother used to say whenever I goofed up, saying "sorry" doesn't make things right.

Bob built last year. He's got a full six acres but dug in right beside me, he claims, to get a flat septic field. (I know about septic, and I know about septic fields, and I know he's pushing my property line, another inch and he'd be offside, so that he can subdivide someday and sell to more Bobs and Cheryls.) After losing mother and my job and all, I had been keeping myself in the house a lot. But once I heard the backhoe digging Bob's foundation, I brushed off my old porch chair. I watched their six-bedroom house being built and I watched them move in. Cheryl and Bob, in their crisp sweatshirts, directing movers all morning and spending an entire afternoon arranging their bent-willow patio furniture. And all the while, thank goodness, Jonathan at the side of the house, lighting his cigarettes with a torched-up butane lighter. Later, Bob came up to my porch and asked me over for a drink. A welcome drink, he called it. As though I was the newcomer.

Cheryl returns from putting the grandmother to bed.

"Mother went down easy," she says to Bob. They both look at me.

"Better round up that dog before you go," Bob pushes back his chair.

I fold my napkin into a tiny square, wipe crumbs from my place, smooth the tablecloth. In the end, I follow Cheryl and Bob to the basement, where Jonathan and Barclay are lying on the couch watching television. Barclay sits up, scratches behind his ear, misting the area about him, including Jonathan, with coarse black-tipped hairs.

"Gotta go," I say.

At home, I undo my shirt and flick on the kitchen light. Barclay whines at the dog food cupboard, so I get his dish (my mother's old porridge pot) and fill it up with dry pellets. When I set it on the floor, Barclay's tail droops between his hind legs. He looks up at me.

"Nothing special on that tonight, old buddy," I say,

"even if it is Thanksgiving. But tomorrow, tomorrow we celebrate with all the fixings, just like always, including giblets and gravy for you." He cocks his head and so, to make him understand, I open the refrigerator and let him sniff our butter-basted twelve-pound turkey that I bought at the A&G grocery earlier in the day. I sure do appreciate family traditions.

PORCH JOCKEY REVIVAL

Our cabin at Happy Sands Resort is pretty much the same as everyone else's. Small, two bedrooms, a combined kitchen and sitting area, a musty bathroom with a powder blue bathtub, sink, and toilet. The toilet has a wooden seat that my husband Geoff and my sixteen-year-old son Alistair say is warm and comfortable. Me, I work with people's bodies. I'm a massage therapist; I know the kind of detritus people shed. Give me cold porcelain any day.

Almost everyone calls me Chiquita even though my real name is Tracy Johnson. Back in elementary school, my mom packed a banana in my lunch. Kids started calling me Chiquita and it has stuck for forty years. I've always liked Chiquita because it makes me sound exotic. In reality, I have white skin, bordering on purple in the winter months, big hands and forearms, and greying auburn hair, usually in a ponytail. In truth, I'm more of an eggplant than a banana.

There is one person at Happy Sands who doesn't call me Chiquita. I don't want you to think she's a senior citizen because I call her "Mrs. Edwards." She's only about fifteen years older than me. Not even sixty yet. But she insists that most people call her Mrs. Edwards—especially people who work for her, like me.

Mrs. Edwards says "Chiquita" suggests insignificance, that it is a derogatory and demeaning nickname. I'll tell you what's demeaning: having to call her Mrs. Edwards.

Speaking of demeaning, Mrs. Edwards has two black porch jockeys at her cabin. The jockeys are three feet high, wearing red caps, red vests, and white jockey pants. One extends a lantern in his right hand; the other extends a lantern in his left hand. They are strategically placed on each side of her cabin door to light the threshold at night. Mrs. Edwards says they are historical artifacts, and that they are "cute."

This afternoon, Mrs. Edwards is on the deck of her cabin, freshening the paint on the jockeys. She does that every summer—makes the whites of their eyes really white and the black on their faces really black. I know by the way she's stooped that she is going to hurt her back and will need a massage. Happy Sands is a working vacation for me. Especially when Geoff is depressed, because if he doesn't blow off the depression by the time we get home, he'll need a leave of absence from his job and we'll be short income.

"How's the painting going?" I ask Mrs. Edwards.

"Fussy," she says.

"That's not a great position for your back," I say.

"I can feel it already. I should book a massage."

"Tonight?"

"You always talk me into it."

Typical Mrs. Edwards comment. How did I talk her into it?

On the way back to my cabin, I pass in front of Kathy's place. She's a single mom who lives just twenty minutes away from Happy Sands, but rents a cabin for her two-week summer vacation. She has four-year-old twins, Tara and Todd. I wonder if she regrets starting both their names with T's. She must. Especially since her ex-husband's name is Terry.

Kathy waves at me. Tara and Todd run out of the cabin in their bathing suits, holding swim masks and snorkels. "Chiquita!" they scream.

"Tara! Todd!" I yell back. Which frightens them because I pack a large voice, but then they laugh. Todd throws his plastic face mask up in the air, landing it on the roof of the cabin. Kathy takes a deep breath.

"Massage?" I ask Kathy.

"Book me in," she says, as she lifts an armload of bright towels and a mesh bag of beach toys from the step.

"I've got the lovely Mrs. Edwards tonight. She's gonna be sore after repainting the racist figurines. How about tomorrow?"

"I'll survive until then. Can Alistair watch Tara and Todd?"

"You bet," I say.

In previous summers, my son Alistair has cheerfully babysat Tara and Todd. He used to smile and be able to engage with all ages. But, as I walk back to my cabin, I'm thinking that Alistair is not going to be pleased that I've committed him to an hour of pro bono babysitting. I'm imagining the pout that I kept catching in the car on our drive to Happy Sands. Bottom lip turned down, zero eye contact, heavy sighs. You'd think there'd been a death in the family. Tough. An hour of babysitting won't kill him. Might even help him. Kathy works twice as hard as anyone I know, especially Alistair who, earlier this summer, found his summer job of pumping gas so thoroughly exhausting that he cut back to three days a week.

It's dark inside our cabin, even though the sun is blazing outside. The curtains are closed. Alistair is watching TV. He's a tall, skinny kid—an ectomorph like his dad, his huge feet hanging off the end of the couch. It is the world's most uncomfortable couch, basically a park bench done up with orange upholstery, and Alistair's angular body makes it look worse. Having tried to stretch out a few times myself, I know that couch is more punishing than relaxing. Why doesn't Alistair move? Why doesn't he lie on the chaise lounge at the beach? Teenagers make no sense.

"Hey Alistair," I say, walking over to the window, "I told Kathy you'd watch her kids for an hour tomorrow."

"Forget it. Those kids are dinks," Alistair says.

"Let the sun shine in," I sing, as I pull apart the curtains and crank open the window.

"I'm too tired," Alistair says.

"Now, honey," I say, "babysitting Todd and Tara couldn't possibly be as hard as pumping gas." I pat his head several times for emphasis. "Could it?"

I walk into the bedroom where Geoff is sleeping. Or should I say, "sleeping," in quotation marks, because this "sleep" is closer to a malfunctioning cyborg state. A blank face, closed mouth, eyes open. Maybe he's not eating enough protein. I wish it were that simple.

"Happy hour," I say. "Do you want a beer?"

"Chiquita, I'm…" he says. And then nothing. The unfinished sentence. The sure sign his inner black dogs have found us on vacation. Somebody should euthanize those beasts. They've wrecked a lot of summers.

I don't have a drink since I still have to work on Mrs. Edwards, but I put The Waifs' *Sink or Swim* on the CD player, barbecue a few chops, and mix up a salad. Geoff and Alistair decline dinner. I eat on the deck, resentful of the fact that, because Geoff and Alistair aren't eating, I feel piggy eating a regular dinner at a regular time.

From the deck, I watch Kathy lifeguarding her kids down at the beach. Tara and Todd play king of the air mattress. They can both swim fairly well, but the air mattress keeps drifting away from the beach and then Kathy has to holler at them to come in closer to shore.

I have a cup of tea. Put the leftover dinner in the fridge in the hopes that Alistair and Geoff will eat later. I don't know what they run on. The two of them are skin and bones. Their Adam's apples stick out of their throats like pebbles.

Mrs. Edwards prefers her massages right after dinner, even though I think that is probably not the best thing for digestion—hers and mine. But a job is a job. I knock. Smile politely at the porch jockeys. Mrs. Edwards, wearing a kimono-type robe, opens the door. I grunt as I squeeze myself, the Moroccan tote bag on my shoulder, and the massage table through the doorway.

Even late in the day, it's still twenty-five degrees outside, and even warmer inside Mrs. Edward's cabin. I push the furniture in the sitting area to one side and unfold the table. Fitted sheet, pillow for under the knees, flat sheet, flannel cover on the face cradle. Then I go stand in the bathroom (she's got a baby blue toilet with a wooden seat, too), so Mrs. Edwards won't feel like I'm staring at her while she disrobes and climbs between the sheets on the massage table. It's a manners thing; I'm going to see most of her nude body anyway. And, honestly, I couldn't care less how Mrs. Edwards looks in the raw.

"Tracy, I'm ready for you now," she calls from the main room.

Yahoo, I think.

Mrs. Edwards is trim but weak. She's the type who will soon have trouble opening jars. She has a flat bum. No glutes to speak of. Lots of people are like this: trim but gooey. You don't have to touch them to know. Mrs. Edwards keeps her underwear on. People are funny that way. I mean, underwear is far more revealing than a bare bum. Mrs. Edwards is sporting a high-rise pair of cotton panties. Plaid. Surprisingly jazzy.

I start on the left side of her neck. Mrs. Edwards has typical middle-aged woman woes: sore lower back, tight scalenes and curved posture—probably brought on by unnecessary stress—lack of muscle tone and poor kinesthetic awareness. I'm the same. Except I have more muscle mass.

I work my way down the sides of her spine until I encounter plaid, which prevents me from doing much work on her lower back and hips. I try my best. I fold her underwear down a bit but the elastic flips it back up with a snap. I focus on her trapezium and finish with a scalp massage, which I haven't tried on her before, because I usually save it as a bonus for people I like.

"I'm not sure I enjoyed whatever you were doing to my head. Pushing your fingers around in my scalp like that," Mrs. Edwards says after her massage, as I pack up my table.

"That's good to know," I say. "Everybody's different. I won't do it next time."

"I feel a headache coming on."

Me too, I think as I stand at the door, waiting to get paid.

"I'll bring your money down to the fire tonight," she says. "I can't find my purse right now."

I'm thinking that she didn't appear to look at all, for even one second, for her purse. But I don't care if I get paid now or later tonight.

"Sure," I say as I heave my stuff out the door.

Almost every night at Happy Sands, someone lights a bonfire in the pit near the lake. Tonight, whoever built the fire has disappeared. Maybe one of the Alberta families with all the kids had a wiener roast and then went to town for ice cream. There are a few tiny lights on the opposite shore, car headlights as a few vehicles travel on the other side. The lake is dead calm, not even the occasional lap of waves, and the warm air is still rising off the beach. I breathe in the heat, along with the summer smells of pine trees and smoke and water. Maybe, I think, Geoff will come for a skinny dip with me.

Geoff is alone in the sitting area of our cabin. "How's the bonfire?" he asks me.

A good sign. A complete sentence.

"No one there," I say. "Mrs. Edwards never showed with my money."

"Predictable," Geoff says. "She likes to yank your chain."

"Skinny dip?" I ask.

"Maybe tomorrow night. I'm tired."

"Nudity might energize you," I say, reaching out, giving his shoulder a rub.

I turn to see Alistair staring at me from the kitchen. He must have been there the whole time, watching.

"Oh, hi, Al. There's leftovers in the fridge," I say.

"Would you just go for a skinny dip with her, dad?" Alistair says. He walks into the bathroom, slams the door, and Geoff and I sit in silence, listening to the water filling the bathtub.

Nights are seriously dark at Happy Sands. There are no street or footpath lights. Only tiny yellow bulbs above each cabin door and, of course, the jockeys' lanterns at Mrs. Edwards' place. The lights inside the cabins filter hazily through the few windows. Most nights, darkness falls hard, and sounds become exaggerated. Tonight, as I lie in bed, I'm sure I hear an animal, probably a deer, walking near our cabin, the sounds of a television from another cabin, kids laughing at the beach.

I give Kathy her massage the following afternoon. She usually pays me in baking, since she doesn't have much spare cash. I see a chocolate cake on her counter and think I'd better give her an extra-special workover. Including a scalp massage, which I know she loves.

Later in the evening, I'm the first to the pit so I light the fire. Kathy and her kids come down for a visit. Kathy has a bottle of wine. A few of the other Happy Sands residents show up: the family from Alberta with four kids, the kissy young couple with a baby, two men who have just pulled up in their boat after a dusk fishing expedition. Mrs. Edwards comes down for a mingle too.

"Tracey," she says. "I've got your money." She holds out a twenty-dollar bill. Flapping it around so everyone can see it in the firelight.

"It's actually sixty," I say, taking the bill from her. "It's always been sixty, and a summer deal at that."

"It's not a deal if I feel worse after the massage." She dangles two more twenties in front of me, one in each hand, and I grab them, stuff all the money into the back pocket of my shorts. I hope she still has a headache.

Kathy fills a plastic cup with wine and hands it to me.

"Makes the power-tripping go down easier," she whispers.

While Mrs. Edwards regales the group around the fire with moralistic anecdotes from her teaching career, Kathy and I finish off the wine. I pop back to my cabin to get another bottle.

"C'mon out," I say to Alistair and Geoff.

"Maybe later," Geoff says.

"Oh c'mon," I say. "People are starting to think I'm on holidays alone."

"Okay," Alistair says, pushing himself out of the orange couch.

"Yeah, you go this time, Al," Geoff says, as though coming out with me is a smelly job to be staggered between the two of them.

Alistair and I sit beside Kathy. I pour Alistair a little glass of wine, thinking maybe he feels in limbo, stuck between the child and adult world, and the wine will be a signal that he can be an adult for the moment.

"Wouldn't it be great if there were two massage therapists staying at Happy Sands?" Mrs. Edwards says loudly, to everyone around the fire. "Maybe someone who does active release."

"We all do active release," I say.

"I'm only saying," Mrs. Edwards says, holding up her palms as though she is making an offering to the crowd, "that competition is never a bad thing."

Alistair is looking at me, eyes wide, the most alert I've seen him in days.

"That's nothing," Kathy whispers to Alistair. "You should have seen how the old bag paid your mom earlier tonight."

Alistair looks at me expectantly. I shrug.

"Do something," he says.

I take a drink of my wine. Alistair stands up, hands me his glass. I watch him walk out of the firelight and disappear into the dark. He wants me to do something? As if he'd be an authority on that. He's probably going to lie down.

I'm up early the next morning and head out for a swim before breakfast. I strap on my goggles, wade in, and, when the water is at my thighs, start swimming. The nights have been warm, as usual, and the water isn't a shock. My system is to swim parallel to the shore until I reach one edge of Happy Sands, then swim in the other direction. This morning, I start with front crawl, then breaststroke, then, before I get to the backstroke, I hear a woman yelling. I slow to a tread and spot Mrs. Edwards.

"Traceeee!"

I dunk my head, swim along the bottom of the lake. She couldn't yell like that if she still had a headache.

"Traceeee!"

I can even hear her underwater. I stand up.

"The jockeys are gone," Mrs. Edwards says.

I look towards her cabin. No jockeys. Hallelujah.

"I want them returned immediately," she says, pointing to the empty spots beside her door.

"Mrs. Edwards," I say. "I didn't take those jockeys."

"It was you. You and your holier-than-thou political correctness. I know what you've been saying."

"What?"

"Check your American history, missy. Those jockeys are a tribute to Jocko Graves, a black boy who helped George Washington."

Sure. And Chiquita is a tribute to Carmen Miranda's hat.

When I get back to the cabin, Geoff and Alistair have arisen from their beds. They're both sitting at the kitchen table, Geoff in his briefs, Alistair in his boxers. The cabin stinks of stale coffee, depression, and unshowered males.

"Anyone want bacon and eggs?" I ask, pulling open the blinds to let in the light of another glorious Okanagan day.

"No thanks," Alistair says.

"Maybe tomorrow," Geoff says.

They can't help it, I think. Geoff is sick. Alistair is a teenager.

No massages on Saturday. After my breakfast of bacon and eggs, I get my murder mystery book, ball cap, and sunscreen.

I sit on the deck and reread the same paragraph three times. The thing is, I don't even care who murdered whom. I'm just reading the book because it's set in Thailand and I've always wanted to go there. Maybe I have a hangover. My stomach feels churny. I wish I had a bottle of water. I doze off for a while. It's going to be a smoking hot day today. Hotter than Thailand. Drier.

Eventually, I finish a chapter of my book. I unseal my sticky body from the chair and go inside. Alistair and Geoff look the same as ever.

"I'm going to go cool off in the lake," I say to the still room. Then I tiptoe across the burning hot sand to the beach.

I am at the water's edge, trying to stuff my hair through an elastic in a ponytail, when Alistair appears. "I'll come," he says, bone thin, in last year's bathing suit.

I offered to buy him a new one at the beginning of summer but he said no, no point. A far cry from last year, when he had to have two pairs of the latest board shorts. I guess that's part of growing up, not getting caught in every trend. And offering to come for a dip with me, even if he's not that keen. The fresh air and exercise will do him good.

We swim to the raft and climb on. Kathy is there, wearing a red one-piece, lying face down. One of her shoulders rides higher than the other, same as it does when she lies on my massage table. I've given up trying to fix that when I work on her. Tara and Todd sit on the edge of the raft, dangling their legs, watching for fish. I join them.

Alistair walks to the end of the diving board and stares into the water. He turns, looks at me. I blow him a kiss. He looks in the water again, gives me two thumbs up, and then blows two kisses back at me. It's the most animated I've seen him all vacation. To top it off, he springs into the air and jackknifes into the water.

The twins squeal at the spray from Alistair's jump. The raft rocks in his wake. Todd runs to the end of the diving board. Stops. "Mom, should I go off like Alistair?" he asks.

"See if I care," Kathy says without raising her head.

Kathy, I think, may have a bit of a hangover herself. The waves from Alistair's jump don't seem to be sitting well with her. Her fingers stiffen, clutch at the boards.

I watch Alistair wade into shore, pick up my towel, rub his head, drop the towel back on the beach. As he walks to the cabin he stops a few times, jerks his head to one side as though trying to get water out of his ear. It is his dad's gesture. My chest tightens at the similarity between father and son, at the power of genetics.

Todd retreats from the diving board, comes back onto the raft.

"Chicken," Tara says, hopping up.

"No, it was my idea," Todd says, catching Tara's arm as she steps on the diving board. Tara swats at him.

"Stop it right now or I'll kill you both," Kathy says.

Todd lets go of Tara's arm, walks to the end of the board. He looks over the edge where the water has calmed since Alistair's jackknife. "Mom," he says, looking past his feet and into the water, "there's a face down there."

"Mm?" Kathy says.

"Mom," Todd says more urgently. "Mom!"

Kathy pushes herself up and walks over to the board.

"Look," Todd points down.

"Let me see," Tara says, running to the end of the board ahead of her mother.

"Oh," Tara says. "I can see the eyes."

Kathy, halfway down the board, peers over the side.

"I can't see anything," she says, first to the water, then to me with a shake of her head and an exasperated why-do-I-have kids? look.

"Try from here," Todd says.

Kathy walks further down the diving board. With the three of them at the end, the board bows into the water. Kathy peers over her children's shoulders.

"There are two faces! It's the jockeys!" Tara squeals. "Mrs. Edwards' jockeys don't know how to swim." She pushes Todd off the end of the diving board. He screams like he's been thrown into a pool of blood. Tara jumps in after him.

Kathy tries to steady herself on the bouncing board, the rocking raft. She carefully turns, takes a few steps.

"Is it really the jockeys?" I ask. I walk onto the board. The water is choppy from Tara and Todd splashing around. I can't see the bottom of the lake.

"Yep," Kathy says, lying face down on the dock again.

The next morning, as I grab a breath in my front crawl while swimming lengths, I see what appears to be a scuba diver from an early James Bond movie. In the tradition of a true frogman, he wears a thick one-piece suit, weighted shoes, and a full-face mask. As he walks mechanically from Mrs. Edwards' cabin towards the water, a scrum of young children, including Todd and Tara, form around him. Hurrying along behind the group is Mrs. Edwards.

"Clear the water!" she calls.

I'm the only person in the water. I wade out to join the kids on the beach.

The frogman stands, wide-legged, taking an overly dramatic pause at the water's edge. With his gloved hand he signals the children and me and Mrs. Edwards to stay where we are. Then he walks into the water, going deeper and deeper. His legs go under, then his torso and the diving canister on his back, then his rubberized head. He completely disappears, except for a few air bubbles, which eventually appear in front of the raft.

A few minutes later, the frogman's head rises in the water. He's coming out. The children are beside themselves with excitement because he has an armful of junk from the lake. He gives each child a souvenir. Tara gets a corroded bracelet. Todd gets a slime-filled Coke bottle.

"My figurines?" Mrs. Edwards asks.

The frogman stands for a moment as if he hasn't heard her, which he probably hasn't since his head is covered by a rubber hood. Mrs. Edwards holds her arm out as though holding a lantern, then she gestures, demonstrating the height of jockeys. The frogman nods, turns and walks back into the water. He returns with one porch jockey under each arm and lays them at Mrs. Edwards' feet. He then bows to the audience, which now contains several adults along with the children. Everyone claps and cheers. One of the Albertans whistles.

"Just a minute," Mrs. Edwards says to the frogman, "I'll get my purse."

I notice Kathy has joined the group; she's laughing with Tara and Todd. It's too bad Alistair and Geoff aren't here. Even from inside the cabin they must have heard all the commotion. I guess they're not up for commotion today.

The porch jockeys lie on the beach. They are wet and sandy, but otherwise in good shape, despite their time at the bottom of the lake. I feel a sense of relief, which, at first, surprises me. And I feel deeply grateful to the frogman, and even to Mrs. Edwards, of all people, for bringing those two jockeys back to the surface.

BREAKING THE MOULD

If tonight's dinner with the Norgay-Hillars is going to be a success, Margaret will have to do all the preparations herself. The hostess with the mostest. She can't complain, she knew the job description when she married David fourteen years ago. In fact, she created the position herself by getting up that first morning in his apartment and coddling him an egg for breakfast. Yes, coddling. And now she's about to coddle the Norgay-Hillars. Again. Every time the Norgay-Hillars phone and report that they are in town, recently returned from a physically exhausting vacation in the exotic locale of blah-blah, Margaret doesn't know how to respond, how to end the call, other than to invite them to dinner. The pattern has been solidifying for more than a decade. The Norgay-Hillars never reciprocate. For all Margaret knows, the Norgay-Hillars live in a tent. A high-end, durable tent, mind you. Surely a tent that has proven itself on Everest.

Margaret doesn't have to look at the *TV Guide* to know about the Blue Jays game. To start with, David was humming after breakfast as he read the sports page. Humming tunelessly, Margaret thinks, like an inefficient refrigerator. Then he left his cereal bowl and coffee cup on the table. No time, apparently, to bus his own dishes. Now he's in the shower—his usual ritual before settling in for several hours of televised baseball. Margaret is certain that David won't give a thought, all day, to dinner, or the Norgay-Hillars.

Tanya Norgay and Edmund Hillar. Even though they have kept their own surnames, Margaret thinks of them as the Norgay-Hillars, a hyphenated couple, tied together with a short section of climbing rope. They once told Margaret that a modern climbing rope could support a bungee-jumping Volkswagen. That is the sort of thing the Norgay-Hillars talk about.

Tidy the kitchen first. Luckily, there are no children or pets to clean up after. That's one thing Margaret and David have in common with the Norgay-Hillars. Child-free. Pet-free. What else is there in common? They all eat. Margaret and David enjoy—about as much as most married couples—their breakfasts and dinners together. But the Norgay-Hillars, Margaret thinks as she stacks dishes, like to eat frequently and heartily, and always together. With their leathery faces and zip-off pant legs, Margaret wouldn't be surprised if the Norgay-Hillars carry a just-in-case stash of trail mix to share for the walk from one room to another. Not that Tanya and Edmund are fat from all their eating.

No, they are far too active for that. They are muscular peas in a pod. Tough people with wool socks and lug sole boots.

Margaret turns on the dishwasher and wipes the counter. She already has the dessert strudel in the fridge. She often makes a strudel for the Norgay-Hillars because it seems so appropriate, something a European hiker might eat after an expedition in the Alps. And for the entrée? Pork tenderloin, she decides. The Norgay-Hillars are carnivores. Pork should give the meal a more professional, less bloody finish than the beef she usually does up for them, especially once the tenderloin is sliced cross-grain alongside Gremolata tomatoes and salad. And her sourdough buns, of course. The Norgay-Hillars need their carbs.

"I'm leaving," Margaret calls as she gathers her purse and her mesh shopping bag that she bought in a craft store in Pincher Creek. She knows David can't hear her over the shower, but she doesn't care if he spends a few minutes discovering that she isn't in the house. Why does he have to shower now when the tenderloin hasn't even been picked up?

"I'm leaving," Margaret calls again, because it felt so good the first time.

She walks quickly through their neighbourhood. It was a simple, straightforward neighbourhood when they moved in a decade ago. All the houses were similar three-bedroom bungalows with an occasional bay window thrown in for variety. Recently though, everything has become cluttered. Tall, narrow houses are infilling the larger lots, people are painting their houses in juvenile primary colours, and cars are parked along the curb so that the street never gets properly cleaned. Thankfully, the strip mall down the street has not changed. There is still a butcher shop and a convenience store.

Selecting the pork tenderloin is easy. "How can I help you today?" the butcher asks in her soft, attentive voice. Margaret is always fascinated by two aspects of the butcher: first, her bleached blonde updo, built on top of her head like a plate of beef tournedos; and second, the way she genuinely seems to want to help. The butcher would be a desirable dinner guest, Margaret thinks.

After she leaves the shop with her purchase, Margaret worries that she should have started marinating the meat last night. No matter, tenderloin will be refreshing for the Norgay-Hillars, who have come back from cycling (had they really said cycling?) in Nepal and probably haven't had pork recently. Or maybe they have. They never talk about the food they eat on these trips but, rather, the height of the summit, the depth of the dive, the vertical slope skied, and the ensuing trauma to their bodies.

For Margaret, a good holiday involves car touring, alone, in Alberta, and perhaps finding a coffee shop or tea room with a homemade soup and sandwich special and a few local crafts for sale. David doesn't like to vacation at all, although he always seems interested in the Norgay-Hillars' sporty escapades. When it comes to outings, there certainly is no climbing rope between Margaret and David. More like a glacial crevasse.

Margaret enters the convenience store. She intends to pick up cranberry juice, since the Norgay-Hillars drink litres of the stuff. Margaret suspects they are prone to bladder infections, maybe from all that peeing in the wilderness, but it is not the type of information the Norgay-Hillars would share. In the store's fridge, beside the drinks, Margaret notices a shelf of ready-to-cook baked goods. Why spend all afternoon mixing and kneading when she can buy her sourdough buns in a tube? The result won't be as good as the sourdough she makes from scratch. Perfect. Then maybe everyone will realize that these dinners take effort.

A teenage boy in a sleeveless T-shirt and with an Afro the size of a beach ball works the cash register. When Margaret reaches the counter, he closes the paperback he's been reading and looks at her expectantly. "At your service," he says. There, Margaret sighs to herself, he'd be an interesting dinner guest. A guest worthy of homemade sourdough buns.

On the way home she reflects upon the first time she and David met the Norgay-Hillars. They were at the university Phys. Ed. ball—sitting together by chance since the tables had filled quickly. After several hours of beer and chatting, the Norgay-Hillars suggested they all go on a weekend canoe trip down the Kootenay River. David was up for it. You wouldn't suspect it now, but before his admin job, David was an athlete like them. Margaret said she would be happy to stay home and read. David had a few beers in him and kept pestering, finally going as far as to say, "It wouldn't hurt to break out of your mould for one weekend."

She didn't go canoeing. David went with the Norgay-Hillars and reported that it rained the whole time. That was years ago—get over it, Margaret thinks as she turns up the walkway to the house. It had nothing to do with breaking out of a mould. It had to do with preferences.

Margaret glances around the yard, which looks like all the other yards used to, before the neighbourhood started xeriscaping. Margaret's yard still has a neat lawn, a shrub patch on one side, a flower bed on the other. If there was time, she'd cut a few Cheddar Pinks and put them in bud vases inside the house. As if anyone would notice.

Margaret can hear the baseball game on TV, and she can hear David snoring—each snore a deep grumble followed by a pause. Now there's someone in a mould, Margaret thinks as she unpacks her groceries as loudly as possible.

After she whisks a balsamic marinade for the tenderloin, she tidies the kitchen. She picks a crumpled dish towel off the kitchen counter. David must have left it there—she would have hung it over the rack. The towel is slightly damp and Margaret is about to exchange it for a dry one when she decides she'll use it to dust the family room, or the "TV room" as David calls it.

She walks in front of the couch where David is sleeping, dusts under the remote control, and then smacks it back on the table. David props himself up on one elbow and tries to peer around her to see the screen. Margaret checks the screen, too. Extra innings, today of all days.

"What are you all huffy about?" he asks.

"Nothing," Margaret says.

"Dinner. You're worked up about Tanya and Edmund even though they won't be here for hours."

"There's a lot to do," Margaret says.

"You invited them," David says.

There is no point responding to such a stupid remark. David will never understand the politics or the orchestration required when it comes to company.

By dinnertime the house is spotless. Margaret has had a bath, thanks to the time freed up by the instant sourdough buns, and changed into her black pants and the sweater with the beaded phoenix. She hasn't worn the phoenix in months—not since David commented that the bird, with all those dark tubular beads at its bottom, appears to have messed itself. Scat, the Norgay-Hillars would call it. Wait, what was she thinking? The Norgay-Hillars would never notice what she was wearing unless it came from the mountain equipment store.

The food will only require a few last minute steps. Tenderloin and tomatoes prepared for the barbecue, baby romaine salad waiting for dressing. The table is set with her antique plates, the pewter napkin rings from High River, and the quaint bun basket she picked up on a car trip to Rosebud.

Even David, Margaret admits, looks pretty darn good. He has put on clean jeans and a navy golf shirt that Margaret recently bought for him. As a bonus, he has tidied the front hall closet.

Margaret opens the fridge and pulls out the tube of buns. She twists the tube according to the directions and raw dough oozes out of the package and through her fingers. She plucks off bun-size bits and sets them on a baking sheet. After burying the empty package in the garbage, she slides the baking sheet in the oven.

When the Norgay-Hillars arrive, they hug as a couple— first David and then Margaret. There are several layers to their coats, including outer shells and inner fleeces. Still, Margaret is certain that she smells the same pine-scented deodorant on both Tanya and Edmund. At the end of the hug, Margaret's phoenix snags on one of the Norgay-Hillars' many coat toggles and there is a brief awkwardness as she detaches herself.

David hangs up the multipurpose jackets, then Margaret leads everyone through the front hall towards the family room, where they will have a drink. On the way, they pass the dining room. Tanya stops talking (about a hot spot she developed on her heel while cycling) to admire the table. Edmund puts his arm around his wife's shoulders.

"Oh, Margaret, you go to too much work!" Tanya cries.

"Indeed," Edmund says.

David nabs a hot bun from the basket. Edmund takes one, too.

"Fabulous," Edmund says through his mouthful as he follows David out of the room.

"Edmund and I are ravenous," Tanya says. "We intended

to go for a short out-and-back in Kananaskis today, but you know us—in the end we'd completed the entire nine-hour loop. Good thing we got an early start."

"Do you ever get sick of each other?" Margaret asks.

"No," Tanya replies.

"Not ever? Don't you ever want to go out alone? Even if it's just shopping?"

"We hate shopping," Tanya says.

"Bun?" Margaret offers.

Tanya peers at the buns and takes the biggest. Margaret notes that Tanya pulls the bun apart in two halves, just as Edmund did, before eating it. No one appears to have noticed that the buns are not homemade.

"Thanks," Tanya says, popping the last bit of bun into her mouth. "I think I'll go see what Edmund is up to."

Margaret adjusts the remaining buns in the basket.

Later, when David, Edmund, and Tanya are seated at the table, Margaret delivers the plates of food. She has been fluttering about the kitchen, trying to convince herself that it makes no difference that the ready-to-bake buns passed as her own from-scratch buns. Now, as she stands in front of her chair at her end of the table, she feels overwhelmed by other irritations. What sort of dining room suite has only one armchair? And why is David always in it? And why are the Norgay-Hillars here at all? Why does she keep inviting them for dinner? Why is she waiting on all these people? The mould, Margaret decides, breaks now.

Margaret takes the edge of the tablecloth in each hand.

She checks the faces around the table—David, Tanya, Edmund, immersed in their three-way conversation about the best way to stretch the quadriceps. Margaret tightens her grip and, stepping back, yanks the tablecloth to her hips.

The table setting jumps toward her. An avalanche of plates and cutlery crash into each other on the way to the carpet. The basket tumbles. Buns scatter. The Norgay-Hillars leap to their feet.

David, looking slightly frightened, asks, "What's with you?"

When Margaret doesn't answer, David comes round to her end of the table. He gets down on his hands and knees and begins cleaning the debris at her feet. Margaret sits in her chair and stares at the Norgay-Hillars. They scurry to Margaret's end of the table, where they crouch and help David pick up the Gremolata tomatoes and tenderloin slices and, of course, the sourdough buns.

Margaret closes her eyes, listens to the threesome working beneath her, and smiles. She has summited.

VACUUMING THE DOG

It was Wednesday and I was vacuuming the dog. The more hair I can get directly off her coat, the less there will be on the floor on Thursday, when I vacuum the rest of the house. Fridays, I vacuum my keyboard because I am a writer. In fact, last month I received a much-coveted government grant for writers. My colleagues were astonished. They'll be even more astonished when they discover that my grant application included a proposal to write a book called *Law and Literature in Canada: From Zero to 2010*.

I take weekends off. On Mondays, I Google stuff. On Tuesdays, I send e-mails. On the Monday before the Wednesday mentioned in the first paragraph, I Googled Richard Posner, the famous American judge who wrote a best-selling book called *Law and Literature*. He also wrote something or other about law and economics. On the Tuesday before the Wednesday mentioned in the first paragraph, I emailed Richard Posner at the University of Chicago and "queried" (as they say in the writing world *and* the legal world—and so the synergy begins) whether there is enough material out there for a book about law and literature in Canada. Ever since I got the grant money I've been wondering about that aspect of my project. Of course, I also hoped that Posner would summarize his books so that I wouldn't have to read them as part of my soon-to-be-started research.

Big judges like Richard Posner probably don't even read their own email, I figured. But nothing ventured, nothing gained. Besides, according to my grant proposal, I had to do research. The grant people must have ways of checking up on recipients. I needed to be able to say, "See, I did more than vacuum the dog—here is a copy of the email I sent to Mr. Posner, AKA Mr. Law and Literature."

As I may have mentioned, it was Wednesday and I was vacuuming the dog. She especially likes to be vacuumed around her neck, and I am always careful not to inadvertently suck up an ear. I have done that once or twice, and she looked at me harshly until I gave her a piece of Gruyère cheese. I explained to her that this vacuum wasn't exactly invented for dog grooming. There is such an appliance. Several years ago, I ordered the PetVac from a flap on the envelope of my department store bill. The photo showed a small hand-held object, about the size of an electric razor. Just the right suction, the ad claimed, to remove loose hair from a dog's coat. However, like the cleaning robot, the musical mattress, and the pomegranate diet pills, the PetVac was a rip-off. It couldn't suck hair off a barbershop floor. I decided from then on I would always be on the alert. If something looks too good to be true, it probably is.

The other place my dog likes to be vacuumed is on her hip bones and at the base of her tail. That's where I was vacuuming Wednesday. "Oh-la-la," the dog seemed to be saying before we were interrupted by the ring of the phone. (I didn't mention the phone ringing at the beginning of the story, even though that is where this story really begins, because that would have been poor style. Like having the story start with an alarm clock waking the protagonist. I've taken writing classes and know a few things. That's why I got the grant.)

"Richard Posner here," the voice said.

Richard Posner said that he had received my email, that he was in Calgary, and that he could meet me for lunch. In an hour.

"For sure!" I exclaimed, eagerly and expectantly (which are unnecessary adverbs that kind of mean the same thing, but I left them in for effect).

Then I remembered the PetVac. If it looks too good to be true, it probably is too good to be true. There was no way on Uranus that this was Richard Posner. But if not Richard, then who? And how had he gotten my phone number? And how would he know that I emailed Posner?

"Do any writing this morning?" he queried.

The truth hit me like a bag of money. This person, this

Richard Posner, was a Canadian government spy working for the grants department. Incredibly, government hacks must have tapped my emails. Now, I will admit that I may have spruced up my credentials when I emailed Richard Posner. I may have suggested that I had written a few books already, which is true—although they are still in the draft stage. I also may have hinted that I had lined up a well-known publisher for my book. Luckily, everything would jibe since my grant application had been similarly spruced.

I suggested that we meet at Timmy Ho's.

"Timmy Ho's?" the *Posner* impersonator queried, as if he was some guy from Chicago who had never heard of the place.

"Yes, Tim Hortons, on 6th."

"All right," he said, after a pause.

What'd he think? I was going to suggest Starbucks and blow my grant money on a venti mocha frappuccino with him taking notes? Mr. *Posner*'s cover was so blown. Plus, that fake American accent was plain goofy. In any event, my dog noticed a squirrel on the windowsill and started barking incessantly. I couldn't hear anything else so I hung up.

I started to put on my best suit. Something I might wear to an important meeting about my trust fund. But then I thought, wait a minute—it can't look like I spent grant money on fancy clothes. Which I did. So I took off the suit, put on jeans, a wrinkly shirt, and sloppy shoes—just like a writer.

I was only a few minutes late, less than thirty. (After all, I had to finish vacuuming the dog's tail.) Mr. *Posner* was waiting outside Timmy Ho's. I knew it was him because he was dressed like a Canadian government employee. Blue golf-style pants, white shirt, glasses. Nice disguise, dummy. I could not discern if he had a microphone taped to his chest, or a camera on his watch.

We introduced ourselves, went inside, picked up trays, and got in the service line. He ordered a bagel with salmon. The most expensive item on the overhead board. But I wasn't tricked. Oh sure, Mr. *Posner* thinks I should buy him lunch with my grant money. That's for subsistence, buster.

"So you have a dog?" he queried as we sat down at a table for two. He picked up his bagel and I tore the wrapper off the pack of crackers that I would be having for lunch. Luckily, before I answered his question, I realized that I didn't want him to think I owned an expensive purebred. Which I do.

"Yes," I said, "a mongrel that I found in the ditch. I eat her food sometimes."

"Dog food?" He put his bagel down on his plate.

"Discount kibble." I emitted a few *"grrrrr"* and *"rrrruufff"* sounds for humour and emphasis.

Mr. *Posner* excused himself, stepped outside the restaurant, and made a call on his cell phone. I imagined him saying, "Case closed. She's legit."

Then he flagged down a taxi and, I assumed, instructed the driver to take him back to the devious government office from whence he came. I finished his salmon bagel.

I returned home and took the dog for a walk. Much later, I Googled Richard Posner, more thoroughly this time, and found a photo and a sound bite. Sixtyish, lean face, horn-rimmed glasses, American accent! Likes seafood!! Apparently, I had been with the real Richard Posner (no more need for sardonic italic emphasis—he's the real thing!) at Timmy Ho's. Whoops. But I'm not the type to cry over spilled milk under the bridge or bygones or corky Cabernet. This is the writing life. Ups and downs. No one, not even me on my grant proposal, said *Law and Literature in Canada: From Zero to 2010* could be written easily in, like, a week. No, I simply call my dog, hoist my vacuum, and begin thinking really hard about a catchy opening line for my book.

LAST SEEN AT TEENY TOWN

As they enter the Okanagan, Matt complains to Kayla that when he was a kid his parents always drove right by Teeny Town.

"You're almost thirty," Kayla says. "I can't believe that still bugs you."

"The sign made me think of it. And besides, it wasn't just Teeny Town," Matt says. "Even though I begged, my parents wouldn't stop at the fruit stand with the petting zoo, or the place with the bumper boats, or even the go-kart track."

"Poor thing. Pull into Teeny Town if you want," Kayla offers.

"Really? Now?"

"Sure. I don't want you complaining about roadside attractions after we're married."

"Oh babe—you won't regret this."

Matt and Kayla met in Banff at the hotel where Matt was the handyman, and where Kayla worked as a summer front desk clerk. At the end of four months—hiking every day off, sleeping in the same bed every night—they got engaged, quit their jobs, and are now on what Kayla calls their *Meet the Fockers* tour. Matt says they can overnight in Penticton where his parents have the largest cabin on the lake. "My dad is a big show-off," Matt has told Kayla. "He wants the celebrity-size cabin, the fastest boat, and the most successful son."

After Penticton, the plan is to stop briefly in Vancouver to make sure Kayla is set up at the University of British Columbia for the upcoming term at grad school, and then carry on for a weekend on Vancouver Island, where Kayla's mom lives in a double-wide trailer with two tabby cats and a hedgehog. "My mom and your dad probably shouldn't sit too close at the wedding," Kayla said. "My mom doesn't do show-offs."

More than seating at the wedding (no date has been finalized but Kayla is hoping for sometime next spring), Kayla has a few other concerns regarding her mother. For instance, she hasn't told her mother about the age difference—that she is eight years younger than Matt. That's something her mother, perpetually negative about men and relationships and life in general, could find upsetting. But Kayla is sure that once her mother meets Matt, and Matt applies his charm, everything will run smoothly. Then Kayla will mention the age difference.

Matt brakes, steers the car between the brick posts, each topped by a stone rabbit mid-prance on its hind legs, that signal the entrance to Teeny Town. There's only one other car—a minivan—in the parking lot, and the building appears to be more of a 1960s urban bungalow than a roadside attraction.

"Doesn't look like much," Kayla says. "And those rabbits aren't teeny. They're bigger than real rabbits."

"Trust me," Matt says.

The front door is propped open with a worn moccasin-style slipper. Straight ahead, a thin elderly woman stands behind a long empty desk. Her grey hair is done in stiff roller-shaped curls, and she wears a frilled blouse tucked into high-waisted jeans. Behind her, in the kitchen, an old man sits at the table, a newspaper spread out before him. He has one thumb looped through his suspender, and he licks the other thumb each time he uses it to turn the page of the newspaper. Kayla flips through the pamphlet on the desk so she doesn't have to watch the licking.

"Busy day?" Matt asks the woman as he pulls his wallet from his back pocket.

"Twenty dollars each," she says. "There's a mom and her kid already touring the exhibit."

"This brochure says ten dollars per person," Kayla says.

"No big deal," Matt whispers into Kayla's hair. "We're here for miniatures, not a bargain. And it looks like these folks could use the money."

He puts forty dollars on the desk, slips his hand under Kayla's arm. Then he gently pulls her through the living room, down a short flight of stairs, and toward the "start" poster, which is above the back door of the house.

Matt pushes open the door and they step into a gravelled compound of small wood huts, like sheds, arranged in a semicircle. The huts are identical, except one has a ladder and a lookout fort attached to it. Matt heads for the first hut on the right.

"Wait—don't I get a vote for which one we see first?" Kayla asks, hustling to keep up with Matt.

"There's an order to these places," Matt says.

"I thought you'd never been to any."

"I haven't," Matt says. "Bear with my childhood fantasy."

"Okay—but it's not like there are numbers, or even signs."

"Listen to your inner GPS for roadside attractions," Matt says, closing his eyes, crossing his hands over his chest.

Kayla laughs, says, "I must not have been outfitted with an inner GPS."

A model train set, laid out on top of a relief map of Canada takes up most of the first hut. Trains loaded with fish circle around the Maritimes. Trains loaded with wheat circle the prairies. And a train loaded with skiers, some of whom have fallen stiffly on their plastic sides, rattles its way through the Rocky Mountains. There's a giant mountain on the west coast.

"That's not a Canadian mountain," Kayla says. "That's the Matterhorn."

"And your point is?" Matt asks.

"Misrepresentation."

"There you go. Thanks to Teeny Town you've got a topic for your paper when you go back to university."

"It's not a paper—it's a thesis."

"Who knew? I'm just a handyman."

Kayla is glad that, as much as she loves Matt, they won't be living together for at least the first part of the school year. She will have time to get her thesis started while he goes north to work as a welder. A welder! A bus driver, a car mechanic, a heavy equipment operator... even a chef at an Italian restaurant in Jasper—all past jobs he has told her about. She is enamoured by the amount of experience he has packed into his extra eight years of living.

The only light in the train hut is a hooded fluorescent—directly over the train set, so it takes a few seconds for Kayla to notice the little girl and her mom standing in front of the display. They are both fair-skinned—the girl is so fair that she almost glows in the light of the hut. The mom is heavy-set—not fat, but plain heavy from the top of her perspiring brow to her swelling ankles.

"Look, press this button," she says.

The girl pushes the button and the train whistle sounds.

"My turn," Matt says, sliding his arm in front of the girl and pushing the red whistle-button.

"You're too old," the girl says.

Matt gives her an exaggerated look of shock, says, "I'm only ten years old."

The girl swats him on the arm. "Liar!"

"You're a smart one," Matt says.

Matt and the girl take turns pushing the train whistle.

Kayla hopes the rest of the huts aren't as irritating.

Once they are all outside the train hut, the little girl steps in front of Matt, stops, stares at him. She tucks her shoulder-length red hair behind her ear in a thoughtful way. It makes her seem older than she is.

"You've got another admirer, Matt," Kayla says, taking his hand.

It seems that Matt picks up admirers everywhere. The other staff at the hotel, tourists, teenagers hanging out beside the river, seniors in coffee shops. He makes people feel good. When Kayla arrived in Banff, Matt was the first person to help her find her room at the staff residence, to show her where to put a few groceries, to ask about her life. Kayla had surprised herself by telling him, at that very first meeting, about how she had been dumped by her boyfriend on the last day of exams, how her marks hadn't been quite high enough to get the provincial scholarship for the upcoming year at grad school, how she had lied and told her mother that she *did* get the scholarship. Matt had made her feel like things would work out. So far, he was right—things were working out. After all, she is engaged to be married. And Matt, her unbelievably sweet fiancé, has promised to help her with money for school.

"Are you someone's dad?" the girl asks Matt.

"Of course," Matt says earnestly. "I have over a hundred children."

"You're lying again," the girl says.

"He's just kidding," Kayla says.

"Kidding is lying," the girl says.

"That's enough, Chelsea," the mother reprimands.

"Sorry," she says to Matt. "She's at that bossy age."

"No problem," Matt says. "We're friends. Aren't we, Chelsea?"

"No," Chelsea says.

"Nothing gets by Chelsea," Matt says. "Must be good parenting."

Chelsea's mother blushes. She says, "I'm just divorced. This is our first summer vacation as a twosome." Then she looks around, says, "I don't know why I'm telling you all this."

"You probably need to talk about it," Matt says.

Kayla recognizes this as one of Matt's favourite lines. He is prepared to listen. He brings people out, but she hopes they won't have to sit down beside a hut and hear this sweaty woman's life story. She seems a bit boring.

The mother doesn't offer any more information, and Matt says, "I mean it. I think Chelsea is smart. Maybe smarter than beautiful Kayla here, and Kayla is the smartest person I know." Matt places his hand on the woman's shoulder for a moment and then strolls on to the next hut. He stoops through the doorway, with Kayla, Chelsea, and Chelsea's mother following him. When her eyes adjust to the lack of light, Kayla sees dolls. Rows and shadowy rows of big, baby-size dolls, floor to ceiling. All behind glass.

"Check it out," Matt says. "Now that's a collection."

"All Caucasian," Kayla says. "Typical."

"You're Caucasian," Matt says.

"I don't claim to represent everyone," Kayla says.

"Neither does Teeny Town," Matt says.

Chelsea pushes the interactive button. An eerie soundtrack of children laughing begins.

Chelsea grabs her mother's arm and starts to cry. The mother says, "I know. These dolls aren't teeny at all. That's what makes them creepy."

"The whole place is creepy," Chelsea sobs.

After the doll hut, the mother and Chelsea apply sunscreen. The sun is directly overhead and there is no shade outside the huts. Chelsea's mother says that they are heading back to the bungalow to see if the old couple will give them a drink of water. Kayla feels the sun pounding off the gravel, feels the sweat soaking through her tank top.

"Ready for the next hut?" Matt asks her.

"Ready to leave," she says.

Matt clutches his hands to his chest. "Where's the love?"

"Overshadowed by my sense of cultural awareness and good taste."

Matt kisses her on the cheek, says, "It's just for fun."

The next hut has a frontier theme. A disproportionately large chuckwagon is parked in the middle of a herd of buffalo.

"Check out the Indians," Matt says, pointing to a hilltop where a number of war-painted figures are propped. "Can I say 'Indians'?"

Kayla surveys the crouching Indians, the straight-backed cowboy dolls—all the usual ahistorical portrayals she's learned about in school—lined up in one disproportional diorama. And then she spots, in one of the hills, a dinosaur. A plastic stegosaurus, small—even smaller than the toy buffalo, and tucked into the hillside, presumably as a visual perk for the studious observer.

"This is horrifying," Kayla says.

"I'm going to say 'Indians,'" Matt says.

"How does this get by anyone?" Kayla asks.

"Not everyone is looking for the same things as you, professor."

A ladder outside the frontier hut leads up the exterior wall of the hut and into the air for several feet before reaching a small fort. Kayla follows Matt, his long legs skipping every second rung. At the top, there's a waist-high wood wall around the edges, and graffiti—racist scrawl, swears, and rudimentary sketches of genitals.

"Guess the owners can't make it up the ladder to clean this," Matt says.

"The owners should be arrested for socio-cultural-geological misrepresentation," Kayla says.

"They're just trying to make a living."

The fort overlooks the parking lot. Kayla watches Chelsea and her mom cross the lot to their minivan. The mom grabs two bottled waters from the back of the van, leading Kayla to assume that the old people didn't give them any water. The mother settles Chelsea in the back seat, then gets into the driver's seat. Gravel crunches as the minivan moves out of the lot and picks up speed to join the highway.

"Looks like we have the frontier all to ourselves," Matt says, putting his arm around Kayla. He cups his hand over her breast. Kisses her.

"You have got to be kidding," Kayla says.

"Nope," Matt says. He slides against her cut-offs, says, "Missy, there ain't nothing Teeny Town about what's in my pants right now."

"No way," Kayla says, pushing him away. "That's not remotely funny."

"Babe," Matt says. "Carpe diem. That's Latin for seize the day… but I'm sure you know that."

"Stop with the 'babe' stuff," Kayla says, backing away from him. "It has always bugged me. It's demeaning."

"Done. No more 'babe.' You could have told me that, like, three months ago."

Matt closes his eyes, spreads his arms wide for a hug.

"Thank you," Kayla says, as she starts down the ladder.

After a silent visit to the hut with northern Canadians building Lego inukshuks and sugar cube igloos, and to the hut with the rotating green felt platform topped with the aluminum Royal Canadian Mounted Police on their musical ride, Kayla and Matt head for the parking lot. They have to exit through the bungalow, where the old couple are sitting across the table from each other, having tea.

"Enjoy your tea," Matt says.

"We've got postcards," the woman calls out. "Two dollars apiece. You can send a note to your friends."

"I've already got one from a previous visit," Matt says.

Kayla looks at his calm expression. No hint of a lie. She marvels at his ability to tell a story when the need arises. Matt glances at Kayla; Kayla mouths, "What previous visit?"

and gives him a conspiratorial wink.

"I thought you looked familiar," the woman says. "Maybe last summer? About the same time of year?"

Kayla almost laughs out loud because there's Matt— caught in one of his white lies. Matt stands perfectly still for a moment, his head slightly tilted as though he's confused, then turns to the woman, says, "Now that I think about it, I was at another place along this stretch. So, in fact, I *could* use a postcard." He puts two dollars on the counter and takes a postcard off the rack. Kayla leans over for a glance at the fuzzy image of a giant stone rabbit prancing.

The man in suspenders says, "I did the words, she took the photo."

Kayla reads "World's Greatest Exhibition" at the bottom of the card.

"Well, when you two tire of running this place you could start a postcard business," Matt says.

The woman beams, "You think so?"

Matt says, "I know so."

At the car, Matt opens the hatchback, tosses the postcard onto the mat, and pulls the cooler towards him. He tugs off the lid and takes out a can of beer. "Want one?" he asks.

Kayla shakes her head no.

Matt pops the tab on his beer, takes a swig.

"Whooee," he says, holding the can in the air. "Here's to Teeny Town."

Kayla watches as he chugs the rest of the beer. Finally, he takes the empty can away from his mouth. She puts her hands on her hips, says, "Did we really just stop here for sex?

Was that your plan? I feel like you had a plan."

"Nothing gets by you university types," Matt says. He squeezes the beer can and tosses it in the cooler, closes the lid with a jerk. "Kayla, no, I did not want to come here for sex in a lousy fake fort. I wanted to see Teeny Town. Okay? I didn't know you were going to bring your piss-ass political correctness through it all."

Matt slams the hatch, gets in the driver's seat. Kayla watches a few cars roar by on the highway. She has never seen Matt this irritated before; the whole summer he has rarely even shown a ripple in his personality, but he is right—she has been pissy. She needs to lighten up. Let stuff go. What kind of road trip, let alone marriage, are they going to have if she picks on every single misrepresentation?

"Hop in, babe," Matt calls. "We'll talk it out."

He seems happy again. Yes, talking it out is exactly what they should do. Kayla gets in the car, closes the door. Matt turns over the engine. Kayla buckles her seat belt. Matt pats her reassuringly on the knee as the car starts to roll forward and the doors automatically lock with a faint thunk.

MRS. GOODFELLOW'S DOG

Mrs. Goodfellow nodded at the dog crate under the kitchen table. "Tipper will be fine in there for the night," she said. "We won't be late."

Vicky set her knapsack on a kitchen chair and even before she had fully knelt in front of the crate, Tipper began a gnashing, snarling bark. Vicky had never been this close to him. She watched his long teeth and mottled gums, but she didn't feel frightened. Rather, she noticed that he was a good-looking dog, a purebred, and she felt sorry that he had to be locked in the crate. Usually, Tipper was in an outdoor pen, but the Goodfellows were having their house painted and the outdoor pen, which was attached to their garage, had to be dismantled for a few days.

Mrs. Goodfellow unlocked the sliding door to the backyard deck. At the sound of the lock, Tipper hurled himself against the metal door of the crate so that the kennel bounced towards Vicky. Clumps of black and tan hair pushed through the metal door.

"The painters were supposed to be finished yesterday," Mrs. Goodfellow said. "But come and see if you like the colour so far. They call it 'mink.'"

Vicky followed Mrs. Goodfellow outside, across the deck. Mrs. Goodfellow had thick black hair, drawn back in a dramatic bun that Vicky wanted to call a chignon, although she wasn't sure if that was the right word. And Mrs. Goodfellow wore an elegant velvet choker around her neck. Vicky's hair wasn't nearly long enough for a chignon, but surely she could find a similar choker at the mall.

"I didn't realize it was getting dark already," Mrs. Goodfellow said. "At least it's been a warm autumn." She stretched her arm towards the house. "What do you think of the colour?"

"I think it suits you," Vicky said, making a mental note to use the word "autumn" instead of "fall."

Mrs. Goodfellow looked puzzled. Then she gave a quick laugh and adjusted her bun. "I wanted ivory. Jack picked mink. One of those 'master of the house' sort of things."

Vicky said, "Oh yeah," and laughed too, even though she didn't know what Mrs. Goodfellow was talking about. Her dad was the man of the house but he couldn't tell the difference between blue and black, let alone mink and ivory.

"Other than Tipper being inside, everything's the same as usual tonight," Mrs. Goodfellow said as they re-entered the kitchen. She raised her voice because Tipper began to bark. "Timothy's up in his room."

The Goodfellows had one son, Timothy, who was almost a teenager like Vicky. Mrs. Goodfellow said that Timothy didn't like being alone in the house, so when the Goodfellows went out, Mrs. Goodfellow hired Vicky. Timothy rarely came downstairs, and Vicky assumed he was embarrassed by his need for a babysitter. Mrs. Goodfellow said he had an entertainment unit in his room and that his headphones were practically glued to his head. She said he favoured classical music at a high decibel.

If he came downstairs at all, Timothy only visited the kitchen. He took a bottle of fancy water from the refrigerator and half a dozen crackers from a metal tin. He muttered "hi" as he entered the room and "bye" as he carried his snack upstairs. From the glimpses she got of his paleness and skinniness, his dark turtlenecks and long hair, Vicky pegged him as the feminine type. The way he whisked the cracker crumbs off the counter, or tensed at the sound of Vicky setting a pen on the table, made Vicky confident that she could put him in his place if the need ever arose.

Vicky wondered why the Goodfellows didn't take Timothy with them tonight. After all, they were going to a basketball game. Mr. Goodfellow owned the team—a women's team, the first of its big-league level in the province. Then again, maybe Timothy didn't want to hang out with his parents. But that wouldn't make sense if your parents were the Goodfellows.

"I'll run upstairs and tell Timothy we're off," Mrs. Goodfellow said.

Her long skirt rustled as she left the room. Vicky thought the skirt was probably made of silk. Mrs. Goodfellow always wore narrow tops and full skirts. Vicky's mother said that was because Mrs. Goodfellow was getting heavy-hipped—proof that she was going to fall apart like everyone else, even though she was rich and beautiful and could make pasta from scratch.

When Mr. Goodfellow entered the kitchen, Vicky was glad he walked right by her and stood at the dog crate. He had the slight, firm body of a gymnast, grey flecks in his hair, a trim business suit. Vicky wished she was wearing something more sophisticated than jeans and a hoodie. Thankfully, since she always had trouble looking him in the eye, he seemed more interested in the barking dog than in her.

Mr. Goodfellow snapped his fingers once and said, "Quiet." Tipper quit barking immediately. Mr. Goodfellow turned around to take his car keys off a hook on the kitchen wall. "Down," he said casually over his shoulder. Tipper collapsed with a thud onto the floor of the crate. Mr. Goodfellow looked at Vicky and raised his eyebrows. He was showing off—but it was impressive all the same.

"Good evening. It's still Vicky?"

"Yes," Vicky flushed.

"Just checking. Sometimes Vickys become Victorias," Mr. Goodfellow said.

Mr. Goodfellow lifted his foot and placed it lightly on the seat of a kitchen chair.

Vicky played with the zipper on her knapsack. Out

of the corner of her eye, she admired the leather of Mr. Goodfellow's shoes. The colour was rich and unusual. Mahogany. Maybe oxblood.

"Have you brought homework to do tonight, Victoria?"

"A bit."

Mr. Goodfellow finished tying his shoe but left his foot on the chair. "I'll bet it's hard to study with all the boys calling you."

There were no boys calling her. And even though she recognized a silly compliment when she heard one, she liked the notion that Mr. Goodfellow thought she was worthy of a name change as well as a few boyfriends.

"Oh, I won't talk on the phone here, Mr. Goodfellow. I don't talk on the phone while I'm babysitting."

"I'm sure you're perfectly conscientious."

To avoid looking at Mr. Goodfellow, Vicky knelt at the dog crate. Tipper stared at her.

"Don't worry about Tipper tonight," Mrs. Goodfellow said as she came back into the kitchen. "A couple of hours in the crate won't kill him."

"The dog is fine so long as he knows who's boss," Mr. Goodfellow said, taking his wife by the arm and opening the door to the garage. "It's all about control."

"The Goodfellows, is it?" Vicky's dad had said earlier that evening as she was packing her homework in her knapsack. "How old is that kid? Is he some sort of fruitcake?"

"I've barely talked to him. Mrs. Goodfellow says he likes to know someone's in the house."

"Why can't he stay by himself? His dad is normal. Big job. Owns a basketball team. Sounds like the wife is overindulging that kid."

Vicky pulled the knapsack onto her back. "Dad, his name is Timothy."

"You call home if Timothy gets creepy with you."

"As if."

The upside to working at the Goodfellows' was the easy money; the downside was boredom. There was no one to take care of, no real babysitting. They didn't have cable TV or popular magazines. Their stereo was high-end and complex, and even if Vicky had been able to locate the power button, she would have been hesitant to turn it on. So, after the Goodfellows left for the basketball game, she unzipped her knapsack, laid out her school books, and set to work at the end of the kitchen table, the opposite end from Tipper's crate. Every once in a while she heard Tipper shifting positions. A few times, when she looked under the table, she could see his amber eyes watching her through the small holes at the back of the crate. She took it as a good sign that Tipper had not barked since the Goodfellows' departure.

After Vicky finished her assigned reading in science and completed a sheet of math problems, she stuffed her books back in her knapsack. She had planned to review the week's notes from her classes, but the math problems had taken longer than she expected, almost two hours, and she didn't want her books on the table when Mr. Goodfellow came home. Instead, she went to the large hall bathroom where there was a mirrored tray that held Mrs. Goodfellow's perfume collection. Vicky picked up a crystal dispenser.

"Conscientious," she thought, spraying the nape of her neck with a light rose scent. Then, setting the perfume back on the tray, she turned on the water tap and stuck her head underneath for a drink. When she turned the tap off, she could hear Tipper whining.

"You thirsty too?" Vicky called from the bathroom.

Tipper whined again. Vicky found a glass, filled it with water, and carried it to the crate. "Poor thing, you've got no water in there."

Vicky tipped the rim of the water glass against the door of the dog crate. Tipper licked the metal bars. He wagged his tail. Vicky admired his slim silver collar. It was more like jewellery than pet-wear.

"Down," Vicky said, testing her command over the dog.

Tipper sank to the floor of his crate. Vicky looked proudly around the kitchen. On the floor beside the fridge there were two empty bowls. Even though they were ceramic, and even though Vicky thought they looked like something French onion soup would come in at a restaurant, they had to be Tipper's. She filled one with water and set it in front of the crate. Tipper raised his ears but stayed on his belly.

Wouldn't Mr. Goodfellow be impressed to see that he was not the only one who could handle a dog?

"Stay," Vicky said firmly while she put her hand to the clasp of the cage door. Tipper started panting. Vicky could feel his breath on her fingers.

"Thirsty puppy," Vicky said as she pinched the clasp open. She stood to one side and opened the door halfway. "There you go," she said. "Drink."

Tipper stayed in the crate. He raised his head and the end of his nose twitched. Vicky swung the door open wide and it clinked against the table leg. The dog's gaze sprang from Vicky's face to the door. Vicky was putting her hand out, intending to prevent the gate from marking the table leg, when Tipper bolted from the crate.

There were two doorways in the Goodfellows' kitchen. One led down a short hall to the front door; the other entrance was the sliding kitchen door which led to the deck. Tipper raced back and forth, front door to sliding door. His nails clacked and slid on the tiled floor. Vicky, recovered from the velocity with which Tipper had left the crate, put her hands on her hips and took a deep breath.

"Here boy," she said, tapping her foot against the water dish.

Tipper veered off his course and lunged at her ankle, driving his teeth through her sock and into her skin. Vicky punched her foot at the dog and scrambled onto the kitchen table. Tipper did not leap after her. Instead, he sat quietly, seemingly happy as long as Vicky didn't try to get off the table. Vicky, cross-legged on the table, pressed her cotton sock against the punctures in her ankle. Occasionally, Tipper took a drink from his water dish while keeping his eyes on her.

"Timothy!" Vicky shouted a few times, thinking that he could help. But Timothy, presumably with his headphones on, made no appearance. Vicky could see the kitchen clock, ticking away the time until the Goodfellows would be home. Not long now. She could see the phone across the room on the kitchen counter. Tipper bared his teeth when Vicky slid towards the edge of the table. Vicky yelled for Timothy again.

There was a bowl of fruit on the table. Not apples and oranges like Vicky's mom kept, but a black wicker bowl with pomegranates and pears. Seasonal and stylish as a magazine cover.

Vicky flung a pomegranate at Tipper. The fruit hit the dog in the shoulder and fell to the floor. Tipper rolled the pomegranate over with his nose and returned his attention to guarding the table.

Vicky dumped the remaining pieces of fruit on the table and waved the empty basket at the dog. Tipper's eyes followed the basket. Vicky flung it down the hall to the front door and, while Tipper scrambled after it, she jumped off the table. She had planned to cross the kitchen and grab the phone. She could phone her parents—they'd come and help. But when she saw Tipper ripping back into the kitchen, she operated on instinct: she pulled open the door to the deck, slipped outside, and slammed the door shut again. No time to grab the phone. Anything to get away from the dog, who was now snarling at the glass.

Vicky studied the exterior of the house for Timothy's lighted room. She found it further along, near the corner and not far from a section of scaffolding left by the painters, so she dragged the scaffolding under the lit window. Her ankle, where Tipper had bitten her, was sore but not bleeding anymore. She moved a cross-board from the lower level of the structure to the top as she hoisted herself up the scaffolding. Standing on the top board, she could reach her hand up to the bottom of Timothy's window. She rapped on the glass. Softly, because she wasn't high enough to get a good solid knock.

"Timothy," she called. "Timothy."

"He probably has his headphones on," said a man's voice from below her.

Startled, Vicky looked down to see Mr. Goodfellow. She pulled on her hoodie, covering the belly skin that had been revealed by her reach to the window.

"Nothing like a classical waltz before bed. Or perhaps he's been mauled to death by Tipper," Mr. Goodfellow said.

Vicky wondered if it was the height that made her queasy. Maybe it was the rose perfume. Or maybe it was Mr. Goodfellow's calm voice.

"I thought Timothy could put Tipper back in the crate," Vicky said.

Mr. Goodfellow hopped easily onto the base of the scaffolding. He began to climb. Vicky steadied herself against the house.

"He's my dog, not Timothy's," Mr. Goodfellow said. "I bought him to watch over my property."

Mr. Goodfellow put his left foot on the board, outside of Vicky's left foot.

"Yes," Vicky said. "He's your dog."

Mr. Goodfellow put his right foot snugly outside Vicky's

right foot. Vicky tilted her pelvis into the house so as not to feel Mr. Goodfellow pushing against her.

"You smell like my wife," he said.

The window above Vicky slowly cranked open.

"Vicky?" Mrs. Goodfellow's voice called down through the screen. "Vicky? We're home. Timothy says you're out here."

"Quiet," Mr. Goodfellow whispered in Vicky's ear. He placed his hands on the house, on either side of her head. His forearms pressed tightly into the sides of her neck.

"I'll go down and turn on the outside lights," Mrs. Goodfellow's voice was distant, as though she had turned her head away from the window. "Timothy, are you sure Vicky's down there?"

Vicky bent her knees and tried to duck under Mr. Goodfellow's arm. He slid his hand down the wall to block her way. Then the side of Vicky's face rammed into the wall as Mr. Goodfellow ground his crotch against her jeans. Her neck felt like it might snap with every thrust.

"Vicky?" Mrs. Goodfellow, now outside, called from the deck.

In the second it took Mrs. Goodfellow to flick on the outside lights, Mr. Goodfellow was gone. Vicky leaned against the wall, breathing into the mink paint.

"Over here," she finally answered.

"Whatever are you doing up there?" Mrs. Goodfellow asked as she rustled across the yard in her long skirt.

"The dog," Vicky said.

"Never mind. Jack is putting Tipper in the garage. We

should have talked more about the dog, about not letting the dog out, I mean."

Vicky ran her fingers through her hair and forced a smile at Mrs. Goodfellow.

Mrs. Goodfellow asked slowly, "Are you okay?"

"Sorry I've made a mess of it this time," Vicky said, starting to climb down the scaffolding, trying not to favour her sore ankle.

"The mess was here long before you," Mrs. Goodfellow said. She brought her hands to her neck and unclasped her velvet choker, letting it dangle like a pendulum from her fingers.

When the Goodfellows separated later that year, everyone assumed that Mr. Goodfellow had instigated the split. They said he was a cad to leave his wife, but a rich and charming cad. Mrs. Goodfellow got Tipper and Timothy, and it was rumoured that she planned to sell the mink-coloured house for a fire-sale price. Vicky's parents claimed they had seen it all coming. After all, Mrs. Goodfellow, nice as she was, had started to let herself go.

And Vicky, well, she decided against buying a velvet choker. Like Mrs. Goodfellow, she realized that she preferred her neck bare.

THE SMILE THAT BITES

Mrs. Waznyk is elderly, going on ninety years old, and people that age get worked up about time. You'd think they'd be good at waiting, since they move slowly, take naps, and generally don't do too much. But when they have an appointment, they want to be punctual or, preferably, early. So I am quite pleased with myself when I arrive at Mrs. Waznyk's apartment ten minutes ahead of schedule.

"Good morning," I say when she opens the door. "Ready for our big day?"

"Don't patronize me," she snaps. "I've had about a hundred checkups in my life."

I smile, because after our cranky trip to the store last month for three-ply Kleenex—never two-ply, even if that's all the store has in stock—I promised myself I would smile every time I felt bitchy. Use the outside to turn around the inside, as my mother used to say. Though, in all honesty, it's not working, because right now I'm thinking, Mrs. Waznyk, if you've had a hundred checkups, why can't you get there yourself? Why don't you take a cab or book the handi-bus rather than recruiting the busy daughter of a long-dead friend?

"I've been waiting quite a while," Mrs. Waznyk says as she picks up her purse from a frail-looking table near the door.

"I'm early," I say.

"No, no, you're half an hour late," she says.

"Now Mrs. Waznyk." I smile hard. "I even wrote it down on a piece of paper for you last month so there wouldn't be a mix-up."

"I have the paper. Here." She opens her purse. It's not a large purse, rather a small beige handbag with two short straps. But, small as it is, it contains a magical number of latching compartments. Mrs. Waznyk opens each one. Click snap click snap. She fingers the items in each section. Finally, amidst the Werther's candies, elastic bands, and twist-ties, she plucks out my note. "Here," she says again. "It says: Julie will pick you up at nine a.m. on Thursday."

I take the paper. Look it over. "It says 9:30," I say.

She takes the paper back. Studies it. "You're not that early," she says.

Mrs. Waznyk slips the note into her cardigan pocket. She unfolds her walker, which has been leaning against the wall, loops her purse straps over her wrist. She shuffles through the doorway, turns, closes the door. Then she opens her purse. Click snap click snap click. She opens and closes each section.

"Can I help?" I ask.

"Just getting the key to lock up." Click snap click snap through the purse sections again. "Here it is," she says, pulling out a green twist-tie attached to a key. She locks the door and plops the key and twist-tie back into her purse.

We slowly make our way down the hall. Mrs. Waznyk's right leg usually takes a decent step, but her left is a dragger. Her wonky gait is emphasized by the pull-up pants she's wearing. I think of them as accidental capris. Eventually we make it to the main entrance of her apartment building where my car is parked in the loading zone. When it comes to driving Mrs. Waznyk, the convenience of the loading zone always overrides the risk of a parking ticket.

I open the passenger door, adjust the seat, raising it so it is easier for Mrs. Waznyk to get out of later. I fold her walker, place it in the back seat. I get in the driver's seat, help her fasten her seatbelt, turn up the heat substantially so she'll be comfortable, turn off the radio because she says music distracts the driver.

We're on our way. This is good. Smooth. In the past, there have been departure complications. A misplaced key causing a lock-up delay before we are even out of the building. An icy sidewalk resulting in agonizingly slow steps to the car. A forgotten shopping list resulting in a full retreat back to the apartment.

Mrs. Waznyk pulls my note out of her sweater pocket while I drive into the downtown core. "You know," she says after looking at the note for a few minutes, "if your handwriting was neater I would have seen that it was 9:30 all along. The 'Thursday' looks like a 'Tuesday' but I deciphered that one on my own."

"They didn't teach handwriting when I went to school," I say.

"That's criminal," Mrs. Waznyk says. She puts the note back into her cardigan pocket.

We arrive at the strip mall where the doctor's office is located. Mrs. Waznyk hands me her handicap parking sign. I hang it on my rearview mirror. Then I get out of the car, get her walker, unfold it, and open her door, setting the walker beside her seat.

"I guess this car suits you," she says, as she tries to push herself out of the seat. "I find it impossible."

"Can I give you a hand?" I ask.

"Not too rough," she says, even before I have taken her hand in mine and put my other hand behind her back for leverage.

Not too rough? It's not like I'm going to haul her out of my car by her ears. What a smile I give her. A perfect Cheshire cat.

"Mrs. Waznyk?" the nurse calls from her desk into the waiting area.

"Yes, yes," Mrs. Waznyk says. She rattles her walker. "Are you coming in?" she asks me. "I need you to remember what the doctor tells me."

"Your memory is fine."

"You're wrong," she says.

"Health care card?" the nurse asks as we approach her desk.

"In my purse," Mrs. Waznyk says. Click snap click snap.

"Perhaps your daughter could help you find it," the nurse suggests.

"She's not my daughter," Mrs. Waznyk says, click snapping through the compartments. "She's my friend's daughter."

After a few more click snaps, I offer to help by reaching for Mrs. Waznyk's purse.

"I just bet you'd like to get in there," Mrs. Waznyk says, turning her body so I am blocked from her purse.

What's that supposed to mean? That I want to get at her money? Like I don't make enough of my own. Good grief. I smile at the nurse, not my turn-around-the-inside smile, but a sideways smile that, when combined with a glance at the ceiling, hopefully projects "This nutty old woman is wearing me down but I'm a good sport about it."

"Aha," Mrs. Waznyk says, proudly handing the card over to the nurse.

The visit with the doctor is short. Mrs. Waznyk doesn't even get undressed. She only takes off her sweater. Underneath she has on a girlish short-sleeved blouse with a yellow stain on the collar. The doctor, a tired-looking middle-aged man, checks her blood pressure. Looks in her mouth and eyes. He politely slips his stethoscope inside her blouse. Listens to front and back.

"Sounds good," he says to Mrs. Waznyk, as he sits down

heavily, pulls his laptop computer onto his thighs and starts typing. "Any concerns?" he asks.

"I don't think my memory is as good as it used to be," Mrs. Waznyk says.

"The brain is an organ," the doctor says, still typing, "that ages along with the rest. Try doing some crosswords."

"Crosswords! You won't be so cavalier about memory when you're my age," Mrs. Waznyk says.

"There are new medications that help. We've talked about them in previous visits. I've got that marked here." He pats his laptop. "But since you don't want to be on any supportive prescriptions…"

"I don't want to be an overmedicated old woman."

"You wouldn't be overmedicated. You would be appropriately medicated."

"That's how it starts," Mrs. Waznyk says. "Yes, that's how it always starts. And in no time at all I'll be on a drooler bus from a nursing home, heading out on a day trips for ice cream."

The doctor sharply hits one key on his laptop, then closes the lid.

"All right then," he says. "I guess that's everything. See you in a year." He leans forward, shakes Mrs. Waznyk's hand, shakes my hand, and leaves the room.

While Mrs. Waznyk pulls her cardigan back on, I calculate that the time spent with the doctor is about five percent of the time I will spend transporting Mrs. Waznyk to and from his office.

"I should have mentioned a little pain I'm having," she

says.

"Why didn't you?"

"These doctors," she says. "They're all on the pharmacy payroll. It's best not to give them any information."

"But you should tell the doctor if you have pain. That's the whole point."

"He's a man. What does he know about pain?"

"Maybe you should try a woman doctor," I say.

"No," Mrs. Waznyk says. "Women shouldn't be doctors."

This is one of Mrs. Waznyk's bizarre opinions, all the more bizarre since she, in many ways, has been a trailblazer for equality in the workplace, having worked her way to the position of manager at an all-male trucking company before she retired. And yet, at the same time, even though she never married, she adopted the title "Mrs." because she felt it gave her legitimacy. And there are certain jobs, doctor, minister, and math teacher included, that she believes should be the exclusive bailiwick of men.

"We'll just book another appointment and come back again if the pain worsens," she says.

Sure, I think. I've got nothing else to do, nothing but chauffeur time on my hands.

"Where shall we go for lunch?" Mrs. Waznyk asks as we leave the doctor's office.

Lunch? I hadn't thought about lunch. I check my watch.

"Oh, I suppose you haven't got time. You're in a rush," she says.

"No no," I say. "Not at all." I don't like to be known as a person in a rush. Not one of those out-of-breath women who feel the need to be involved in everything from the office steering committee to the Christmas party planning team to the next 10k charity run for the next illness or newest children's helpline. But I think it's important to volunteer, to help others. That's pretty much why I'm here. That, and the fact that Mrs. Waznyk doesn't have anyone else to drive her around, so I'm stuck with it. But old people take forever to eat a meal and I do have a few other tasks to accomplish today. Groceries, library book return, and I'd hoped to go for a workout on the elliptical machine. It's my day off work and I don't want to waste it.

"How about a coffee?" I suggest as a compromise. "At Tim Hortons. There's one next door."

"Do they have soup? I want hot soup."

"They have soup."

I'm excited by my own genius. Tim Hortons is next door, mere steps away. We won't have to add an extra in-and-out of the car episode, we won't have a two-hour meal, and I can get one of those honey crullers that I like.

Tim Hortons is crowded. Because the service line is long, likely too much standing for Mrs. Waznyk, I settle us into a table for two before ordering. Her eyesight isn't great, even with her saucer-size bifocals, so I read her the items from the menu board, skipping those that seem inappropriate. I'll lose her if I read off everything. Besides, she couldn't possibly want a Chili Combo or a Chocolate Brownie Iced

Capp. She said she wanted soup so that's my main pitch. It works.

I leave Mrs. Waznyk at the table and line up to place our orders. In front of me is a woman in knee-high black boots and a slim-skirted business suit. She has a lilac scarf around her neck, casual, and yet just so. On her hip she holds a darling child, a toddler. His hair is a bundle of loopy black curls, like hers, framing big-lashed eyes.

"Jeremy, how about a maple donut?" she asks him.

Jeremy shakes his head, no.

I love that name. Jeremy.

"Now a maple donut would be best," she says. "Mommy wants a taste."

"No," Jeremy says.

He lays his chubby hand on her cheek. She gently takes his wrist and puts his hand back on his chest. She sways and hums a tune, something from a children's entertainer, probably. I don't have kids so I don't know any of those chipper ditties. Thank goodness.

I glance over at Mrs. Waznyk. She has opened her purse on her lap and is click-snapping for something. Even from this distance I feel the urge to rip the purse out of her hands.

The line inches forward. When the attractive woman reaches the counter she orders a coffee and a maple donut.

"No," little Jeremy says, and tries to squirm out of her grasp. Wouldn't he just like to take a roaring trip around the tables, or maybe trot right out the door and onto the street? She has to hang onto him.

"Sweetie," she says, tightening her hold. "Please don't.

Mommy will set you down when we get to the table."

A man sitting nearby, noticing her trouble with a wriggling child and a hot coffee and a maple donut, and no doubt noticing her looks, jumps up—and I do mean jumps, like a complete jackass-in-the-box—and carries her order to the empty table right beside ours. He's in an expensive dark suit, the fabric not unlike hers, and he dotes on her for a few minutes, getting her a napkin, sliding a chair up beside her for Jeremy. The man winks and waves at Jeremy several times before returning to his colleague. Jeremy, his lip jutting out in the sulk of all sulks, sends the man a couple of eye daggers.

As I carry my tray with my order back to our table, I see Mrs. Waznyk has sunk into her chair as though her back is a wet noodle. Her legs are spread apart, one orthopedically-clad foot on either side of her chair. She has pulled out the note from her pocket. The 9:30 note. I hate that note.

"Want me to throw that out?" I ask, setting the tray in front of her and reaching for the note.

"No thank you," she says, stuffing the paper back in her pocket. She looks at the tray. "Took long enough. Isn't there a bun?"

"I guess not," I say. I pull my cruller from the tray, settle into my chair.

"I'm sure you said the soup came with a bun."

I'm watching the woman in the suit. She is reaching out her arm and making *gootchy-goo* sounds and gestures to Jeremy. Well, I think, if anyone can pull him out of his funk, that mother can.

"If we paid for a bun, we should get it," Mrs. Waznyk says.

"I'll get your bun," I say, and then I smile so fiercely my upper lip might split open like a fighter's. I'll get her goddam bun, all right.

The line has gotten longer. Forget it. I walk to the end of the counter where the Tim Hortons employees are putting together orders. I pluck a bun off one of the trays prepared for another customer.

"There," I say, slapping the bun down beside Mrs. Waznyk's soup. "There's your bun." I know she will be offended that it isn't on a plate, that I have used my fingers, but it all makes me feel more satisfied than rude.

Mrs. Waznyk picks her purse off her lap and sets it on the table.

"I want to give you some money for this," she says.

"Oh no," I say, "My treat."

She reaches for the first latch. I don't think I can bear another purse search.

"You buy next time," I say, putting my hand on top of her purse.

She pauses, looks at me steadily, then jerks the purse out from under my hand and sets it back on her lap. She picks up her spoon and tastes her soup.

"Could be hotter," she says.

Jeremy's mother tears off a piece of the maple donut and pops it into her mouth. Jeremy starts to cry. His mother tears off another piece of donut and holds it out to him. His chest rises as he sucks in a colossal amount of air, his face screws up in a pre-wail. Oh no, I think, a screamer. Luckily, before he makes a sound, his mother picks him up and sets him on her lap. She whispers in his ear. The screwed-up face collapses, the crying stops, Jeremy hangs his head. Wow, I think, she's good at this.

"How's your job?" Mrs. Waznyk asks.

"Fine," I say. I'm eating my cruller, watching Jeremy and his mother.

"What is it you do again?" Mrs. Waznyk asks. "I can never seem to retain that."

I'm thinking, do we need to discuss this again, now? I glance away from Jeremy and his mom to look at Mrs. Waznyk. She is looking at me expectantly.

"Consult. I'm an oil and gas consultant," I say, with a good measure of finality, returning my attention to Jeremy and his mother. But Mrs. Waznyk charges on, determined to make a conversation.

"I thought you were an engineer."

"I am an engineer."

"My, isn't that something. Two jobs."

Jeremy's mother puts the piece of donut, the one she tried to feed and cajole him with, into her own mouth. Good move, I think. If the little stinker won't eat the donut, eat it yourself.

"You must work long hours," Mrs. Waznyk says.

Jeremy twists, quick, and slaps his mother's face. She takes his hand, firmly bringing it to his side. She takes a sip of her coffee and then says, "Please don't hit mommy."

I'm impressed. Her brow doesn't wrinkle. Her jaw

doesn't clench. The two businessmen at the table beside her have stopped talking. The jackass-in-the-box looks ready to spring to her assistance again. There's a full table of women nearby who have switched from animated chatting to whispering.

"Here," the mother says. She tears off another piece of the donut and holds it in front of his mouth. Forget it, I think, he doesn't want the donut.

Jeremy seals his lips, kicks his legs. To my relief, probably to the relief of everyone in Tim Hortons, since most of us are watching, the mother sets the piece of donut neatly back on the plate. Who, after all, wants to be force-fed a donut? The mother turns Jeremy on her lap, so he is facing her directly. And then, as my thoughts are turning to Mrs. Waznyk's comment about my long hours, thump, just like that, Jeremy's mother punches him in the chest. Not a playful punch. The real deal.

Mrs. Waznyk, who I thought was focused on her soup, says loudly, "Something's not right at that table," and nods at Jeremy and his mother. I wish Mrs. Waznyk knew how to whisper. Of course something is not right at the next table. That mother punched her kid.

"I take every third Friday off," I say. "It's one of the perks of consulting."

"I said," Mrs. Waznyk practically yells, "something's not right over there."

"There, how do *you* like being hit?" the mother asks Jeremy. She's talking in a low, soothing voice. "Do you want to know how I feel?" She winds up and punches him again.

"Do you like it? Do you?"

Tim Hortons is so quiet you can hear the jingle of the zipper on Jeremy's hoodie after the second punch.

"Now," his mother says, "you can sit back on your own chair and we can share our maple donut."

Jeremy sniffles. His mother sets him in the chair beside her. She looks around at the other customers, at first demurely, then flashing her perfect teeth like a celebrity working the paparazzi. The two men in suits stand up. On their way out of the restaurant one of them, the one who had paid attention to Jeremy's mother, crumples his napkin and tosses it into the garbage bin. Two points, he says. The other man laughs.

"Shameful," Mrs. Waznyk says. "People are shameful."

As the regular hum of the coffee shop returns, I walk to the service counter, stand in line, ask for a small plate. I take the plate to our table and slip it under Mrs. Waznyk's bun.

"Thank you," she says. "That's service with a smile."

I look over at the table where Jeremy's mother is lightly adjusting her scarf, gathering up Jeremy and her purse, getting ready to leave.

"Bon appétit," I say.

MARKING TERRITORY

Paul slid his hands down the railings towards the basement
and then jumped half the stairs. He turned to look at Louie,
the Dachshund, who shivered at the top of the stairs. Paul
climbed back up, tugged at the dog's collar.

"Come on. What's the matter?" Paul started to drag
Louie over the first step. Louie nipped at Paul's wrist and
scuttled across the linoleum to a corner behind the kitchen
table.

"Crazy dog," Paul said, thumping down the stairs by
himself. On the bottom step he picked up a large flashlight.
He remembered the flashlight from his walk-through
prior to buying the house and was glad the realtor had left
it behind. The emptiness of the basement made Paul feel
uncomfortable, exposed. He ran the circle of light around
the empty room and windowless walls. The foundation was

wood rather than cement, and the room had been framed and wired, but not drywalled. Two bundles of wires hung from the ceiling.

Paul walked across the gravel floor and knelt to examine one of the electrical outlets. The wiring was fine, sufficient to support his beer fridge. He had expected much worse, since the realtor had rushed him through this part of the house. Possibly, Paul thought, the realtor was rushing so Paul wouldn't notice the rancid, yeasty smell in the basement. Paul had noticed it right away—who wouldn't? But he figured the smell was insignificant in his grand scheme of country home ownership.

Indeed, before the realtor had even opened the front door of this house, Paul had pictured himself on the deck, with a beer, cooling down after dropping a few trees for the winter wood supply. The surrounding foothills gave him the warm fuzzy feeling of big property, big personalities, and big toys. Of course, Louie, his wiener dog, didn't exactly fit in. Paul would have preferred a Shepherd or a cattle dog that would travel in the box of his truck rather than on his lap. But he was stuck with Louie since the dog belonged to his daughter Cassandra. When Cassandra was just a toddler, Paul bought her the dog. It was beyond him why, at the SPCA, she picked the most pathetic male to adopt.

Paul shone the flashlight along the corner where the floor met the wall, illuminating a small pile of dirt and twigs and old leaves where the odour seemed to be coming from. He walked quickly around the perimeter of the room and, with his light and his nose, discovered several more rank piles. He'd clean them later. No sense dealing with them today. He should go back upstairs to check on the dog, shovel the spring snow, make a cup of coffee, floss.

"Lots of land," the realtor had said when Paul was looking at the property. "You keep horses?"

"No, just a dog."

"Family?"

"Divorced. One teenage daughter."

Cassandra lived in the city with Paul's ex-wife. In addition to excelling at her job as a writer of parenting books, Paul's ex-wife cooked gourmet meals, coached community sports, did her own tax returns, and was a competitive triathlete. At forty-five, she was still a hottie. But even so, when she asked Paul to move out, he felt the relief of a second-string player, forever in the shadow of a healthy and talented front runner, being released from the pressures of competition.

Paul hustled up the stairs and returned to the kitchen. Louie trembled under the table. Paul coaxed the dog out with a Cheezie. When Cassandra was around, Paul hid the Cheezies bag. "No snacks," Cassandra insisted. "Dogs should eat dog food." Paul liked the secret Cheezies. He felt they gave him an edge, if not complete control, over Louie.

"Scared of the basement?" Paul asked. He threw the dog another Cheezie and ate one himself. "You big sissy."

"Louie, I'm home!" Paul called, a few days later, as he entered the house and set down two cases of Big Rock beer—the first supplies for his newly connected fridge. Louie whimpered into the hallway.

"What's the matter?"

One of Louie's long ears was flipped back, exposing the soft pink interior. Paul glanced around the room. On the landing, just in front of the stairs to the basement, he saw several wet heaps of dog diarrhea.

"What the hell's the matter with you?"

"Hardly need to build a dog run for a wiener dog."

Paul turned from digging a post hole to see a man on an enormous black horse. The bottom of a military-style haircut was visible between the man's cowboy hat and the upturned collar of his jacket. His horse exhaled plumes of frosty spring air from coaster-sized nostrils.

"Ought to just stick him in a shoebox," the man said, and pointed at Louie, sleeping soundly in a soft bed of needles under a spruce tree.

"I like to know he's got lots of room." Paul tried to sound light-hearted. With only half a hole dug, he was already discouraged by the effort it was taking to break through the cold ground. There was no way he would admit to this new guy that he'd been cleaning up dog diarrhea every day— that's why he was building the run. He couldn't leave Louie alone inside anymore.

"Hal Ward. Third right on Range Road 54, just before your turnoff. This here's the General." Hal walloped the horse on the neck before extending his hand to Paul.

He continued to talk while shaking hands. "Nice to have someone regular move in here. The last owner of this place was that woman with the mountain lion. Fancied herself an animal trainer. A real fat-assed Jane of the Jungle."

"I haven't heard anything about it."

"Ask around. She was a piece of work."

"The woman or the mountain lion?" Paul asked.

"They were both nuts. Typical." Hal maneuvered the General around and took a last look at the sleeping Dachshund. "Does quite a job guarding your place, eh? Is he drugged or something?"

"Just tired. He doesn't sleep well in the house."

"Poor baby. I got a rifle that would fix that."

The local vet lifted Louie onto the examining table. Louie stared at the vet's bright paw-print shirt, as though searching for his own tiny mark among the oversized dog tracks.

"With an animal of this size, I'm sure I don't have to give you my lecture on dogs riding in the back of trucks."

"No. He won't ride in the box."

"I got a Bull Mastiff in yesterday," the vet gestured towards a door marked "SURGERY" behind him. "Wasn't even thrown—just slammed into the cab at ninety clicks when idiot-boy jammed the brakes."

The vet put his stethoscope against Louie's side, listened, and then looked up.

"Something racing through here. Probably beaver fever. Or could be stress. Is the dog stressed?"

"In the house. Especially near the door to the basement."

"New surroundings. That might do it."

"Did you ever hear about a mountain lion that lived in

my house?" Paul asked.

"Yep. By the time I saw her, I had to put her down." The vet shoved a gloved finger under Louie's quivering tail. "Diagnosis: prolonged misery. Death by basement. You can't keep a cat in a situation like that." He snapped off his glove and set Louie on the floor. "Had to drive up to the house to do it. I was scared shitless, but that old lioness didn't even stand up. She looked bored."

Hal Ward drove slowly up the middle of Paul's gravel driveway. His three-quarter-ton truck had the longest box Paul had ever seen. Long enough, Paul thought as he watched from the empty woodshed that stood beside his house, to ferry a little truck like his own.

"Play poker?" Hal asked, shifting his truck into neutral and resting an elbow out of the open window. Paul set his chainsaw down. He had been reefing on the starter cord without results. Each frustrating yank had brought him closer to driving to town and buying an expensive bundle of pre-cut firewood at the hardware store. Blisters were rising on the fingers that held the starter cord.

"Not much."

"We lost Larry O'Shea when he went on the wagon."

"I guess I could play." Paul glanced at the pus bubbles on his fingers and shoved his hands into his pockets.

"Friday night. May as well meet here since you don't have a missus." Hal nodded at the chainsaw and added, "Check your spark plug."

"Oh thanks, I suppose Friday's all right. But not too

late—my daughter's coming on Saturday and I was hoping to get things organized." Hal's truck started to roll back down the driveway before Paul finished speaking.

Paul, Hal Ward, and Bud and Stu from the other side of the highway sat around Paul's kitchen table. Bud and Stu were brothers whose local fame was sealed when they sold off their Longhorn cattle and bought a herd of buffalo. Hal introduced Bud and Stu as the Bison Brothers. They both wore green baseball caps. Paul ran his hands through his thick hair—a long-standing nervous habit—until he felt Hal staring at him in annoyance. Paul quickly returned his hands to his cards.

Bud tossed out the last card of the deal, squared the remainder of the deck with his beefy hands. He slapped the deck in the centre of the table.

"Hey Paul, did that woman leave anything weird around the house? Any sexy stuff?" Stu asked.

"Not that I've seen," Paul said.

Hal picked up his cards, swore, then tossed the cards on the table and stood up. He re-tucked his pressed shirt into his jeans and started towards the stairwell.

"I'm out. Beer's down there? Who else needs to reload?" Hal pointed at the empties on the table.

Stu and Bud each held up two fingers.

"Flashlight's at the bottom of the stairs," Paul said.

"Could use a few more lights down there," Hal said after taking a few steps and pausing. "Why keep the goddamn flashlight at the bottom?"

"Seems to be plenty of light coming down from the kitchen. Scared of cellars?" Bud asked.

"Don't wanna break my friggin' leg. Is that all right? Is self-preservation all right?"

When Hal came back up he was sweating and holding an armload of beer. He glared at Paul.

"City Boy, there's still territory piles down there. Why didn't you clean that up before you spent time building a dog run for the wiener?"

"Territory piles?"

"Mountain lion crap. Piles of twigs and dirt that the mountain lion pisses and craps on."

"Oh," Paul said. Who knew? After spending everything on this house, why hadn't he bothered to clean those piles up yet? Mainly, he decided, because he hated being in the basement. It wasn't that he couldn't take bad smells, and it wasn't as though he got diarrhea like Louie, but surely, if even a big bull like Hal Ward got sweaty and ornery down there, it was understandable that Paul, too, might be nervous.

The poker game went on until three a.m. Hal Ward took about $50 off everyone. Paul flopped into bed as soon as they left. Cassandra was dropped off by her mother a few hours later while he was still sleeping.

"What stinks?" Cassandra asked when Paul showed her the basement. She stood on the gravel floor while Paul stood on the bottom step, creating the illusion that he was the same height as his tall daughter.

"Those piles." Paul felt he might alarm his daughter if he gave her any information about the previous residents.

"Why don't you clean them up?" Cassandra asked with a sniff.

"I don't really notice them," Paul said. He ushered Cassandra back up to the highlight of the house: her room, a wood-beamed loft that overlooked the kitchen. Then he pointed out the bathroom, which he also wished he'd cleaned, especially after the Bison Brothers had used it. While Cassandra stopped in the bathroom, Paul gathered a broom, a garbage bag, and a dustpan and started for the basement.

"Paul?" Cassandra yelled before he reached the second step. "You got any tampons?"

Cassandra started calling Paul by his first name when she was thirteen. Even now, after three years, he was not comfortable with it. He never said anything about it to Cassandra because his ex-wife had written in her latest book that calling parents by their first names was a healthy sign of a properly progressing adolescent. Probably yelling about tampons was a good sign in his wife's books, too.

"Well, do you?" Cassandra called again. "You know, leftovers from a girlfriend or something?"

"No. No girlfriend. I'm on septic here. Don't flush any of those things down the toilet."

"Mom says you have issues with females."

Paul continued to the basement, wondering why Cassandra called her mother "mom" but wouldn't call him "dad." He swept the stinking piles into the dustpan and dumped them into the garbage bag. He twisted the bag to shut out the smell and lugged it up the stairs. In the kitchen, he stopped to readjust his grip. The smell was so intense that Paul checked the bag for holes and then twisted the top again. A hot gust of air swept by the top of the bag. Louie yelped like he'd been shot. The front door of the house banged. Some sort of weird draft, Paul thought.

Paul emptied the bag into the firepit in the backyard. He squirted an arc of lighter fluid on the pile and tossed on a match. Cassandra joined him as the initial tower of fire settled into a steady flame. She lifted her heavy black boot and kicked at a boulder on the rim of the firepit.

"Give me the truck keys so I can drive to town and get some tampons."

Paul pulled the keys out of his pocket and tossed them to her. He didn't think she was a very good driver, having only recently gotten her license. But he didn't want to leave the fire, and anyway, he didn't want to take her on that particular errand.

"Don't ride the clutch," he said.

A minute later, he watched the gravel fly as Cassandra fishtailed his truck down the driveway.

Paul's property included a high ridge on the east side which sloped into a valley on the west side. The realtor had told him it would take about half a day to walk around the fence line. Paul planned to walk it today, Sunday, with Cassandra and Louie. There would be wet snow to trudge through in spots, but it was a warm early spring day, perfect for walking.

Cassandra was happy to go along for the tour; Louie refused to leave the deck. Ignoring Cassandra's disapproval, Paul laid a row of Cheezies on the deck and down the steps onto the driveway. Louie ate his way across the flat surface, but stopped at the stairs.

"Why don't you let him stay here?" Cassandra asked. "How's he going to keep up with us on those two-inch legs?"

"It's the principle," Paul said as he attached a leash to Louie and tugged him down the steps. "First, he hates staying in the house. Now, since I cleaned up the basement, he won't go in the yard. Someone other than a wiener dog has to be the master around here."

Paul continued to pull the leash until one of Louie's black nails caught on a split in the wood, and he yelped in pain. Cassandra scooped the dog up in her arms. She wiped blood off the torn nail with the cuff of her sweater.

"Satisfied, tough guy?" she said to Paul. She put Louie in the house.

As he walked away from the house, Paul took a deep, satisfied breath. They were going to walk around his land. Just his name on the title. He turned to Cassandra. She wore an oversized red sweater and loose jeans, and she looked pissed off. Paul would've liked to give her a hug, partly by way of apology about Louie's nail, partly because he loved her, and partly because he felt happy with his property. But Cassandra kept her distance behind him.

Paul chose a trail that ran parallel to the ridge, underneath the uppermost rock outcropping. He pointed out the distant roof of Hal Ward's horse barn, and further along, the buffalo moving across a rise on the Bison Brothers' property. Cassandra nodded but didn't respond. Paul left her to her silence and began mentally planning projects for when he finished the dog run. Fencing, for the animals he would acquire. A horse to ride for checking the fences. Mosquito netting around the deck. Bird feeders with squirrel busters on the bottom.

His plans were interrupted when Cassandra tapped his shoulder. She pointed to the outcrop. Paul studied the stubby trees and jagged rock. Nothing. He shrugged.

"Don't you see the mountain lion?" she asked.

"Are you sure?"

"Of course I'm sure."

"Let's get out of here," Paul said. "Those things are unpredictable."

"Do you want to see my deer impersonation?" Cassandra spread her hands above Paul's head to make antlers. "Heeere's dinner!" she called to the ridge.

Paul grabbed one of her upper arms and squeezed hard.

Cassandra twisted free and tossed her hair. "Get over yourself," she said, and resumed strolling down the trail.

Paul watched the packed snow plopping from the base of Cassandra's big boots. Sulky teenager. Get over himself? What was that supposed to mean?

Paul looked up to the outcrop again. A slight movement caught his eye. Feline and feminine. The silhouette of a cat was on the ridge, undeniably huge.

By the time they reached the house, Paul and Cassandra

were walking side by side. As they stepped onto the deck, Hal Ward rode up the driveway on the General. Hal brought the big horse to the edge of the deck.

"Larry O'Shea's off the wagon. Now that he's drinking, we don't need you as a poker fourth anymore," Hal said.

"This is my daughter," Paul said.

Hal tipped his hat at Cassandra. "Best you keep her away from the local wildlife," he smirked.

"Like the mountain lion we saw today?" Cassandra asked, with wide-eyed mock naïveté. Paul noticed she even threw in a hillbilly inflection. Hal shifted in his saddle.

"Now that's rare. A big dog, maybe?" Hal directed his question at Paul.

"No, a mountain lion," Paul confirmed, "on the ridge." As Paul spoke, the General released a steaming fountain of diarrhea.

"Be in touch," Hal said, tipping his hat again and turning the General down the driveway.

"Look," Cassandra laughed, pointing down the hall after they had hung up their coats.

While they were out, Louie had tipped over the garbage in the bathroom. A used tampon, partially wrapped in toilet paper, lay between him and the bathroom door. Louie was growling and backing up against the bathroom cabinet, trapped by the tampon.

Cassandra said, "Looks like he can't relax in his own territory either."

Paul said, "Stupid wiener dog.

HYDROCYST

Saturday afternoon. Lola has left her packing list on the kitchen table: squash racquet, snowboarding pants, two swimsuits, volleyball knee pads. I walk to the sink, look out the bay window, remind myself that Lola is eighteen. She doesn't need my input. Probably things have changed since I went to university. Still, it's hard to imagine there will be time for all her extra-curricular activities during first year engineering.

From the bay window I scan the treed slope in the backyard. Lola and I live on a forested edge of the city and, like our neighbours, we haven't fenced our yard. It gives the illusion of acreage living. Our neighbour, Brad, has built a deer feeder—a wooden manger full of hay—and the mule deer have worn a path that traverses our yard and ends at his feeder.

"Hi Mom," Lola says, flip-flops snapping as she enters the kitchen. "Do you have any spare shampoo? I'm out."

She leans over the table, picks up the pencil, scribbles on the list. Her low-slung sweatpants don't exactly show her crack, but they certainly hint at it. Butt cleavage. There's no sense commenting. She leaves tomorrow.

"Take whatever you want from the bathroom," I say. "There's a spare tube of toothpaste under the counter. And cream. Take it all." ·

"Thanks. I only need shampoo."

I suppose those are the pants she'll wear around the residence at university. Maybe she'll wear a longer shirt, not the tiny, tight one she has on now.

"I'm going to put a load of laundry in," Lola says, tossing the pencil into the air, catching it between two fingers.

"I'll do it for you," I say.

"That's okay," she says.

I hear her gathering clothes in her upstairs room, then coming back down the stairs, through the kitchen with an armload, and into the laundry room off the hall. Even though I've spent years training her to do her own laundry, I want to do it this time. A leaving-home present. A way to check on the state and nature of her underwear. A way to feel more involved in the process of her departure. So far, my only jobs are to keep quiet and drive her to the airport tomorrow.

I check Lola's list again. She's added "hiking boots." I can't help myself. I call into the laundry room.

"Honey, do you think you'll have time for hiking trips

at university?"

"You betcha, Mom," she says. I hear the lid of the washer shut, the ratcheting sound as Lola sets the dials.

My friend Janet phones me as I start the kettle for another pot of tea. "Has Lola gone yet? I tell you, I was sure glad to see the back side of Kyle last week. His little emperor routine was driving me nuts."

"Tomorrow morning. She's not driving me nuts."

"Oh, come on. It's a biological thing so that we're happy to see them go."

"She has a stupid packing list."

"She'll be fine," Janet says. "The kids are always fine."

While there are many deer that cross the slope on their way to Brad's place, these days I watch for one doe in particular— the doe with the growth between her forelegs.

I first noticed her in June when I was looking out the window and mulling over Lola's high school graduation ceremony (where Lola and I had been an inadequate twosome amidst all the cheering family support-pods). One deer had paused, interrupted my mulling by turning away from the poplar stand on the slope, tentatively making her way toward my house. She came right down, stopping to forage on the long blades of grass at the edge of the deck. I could see a round lump about the size of a baseball growing on her chest. Her ears flicked, and then, lifting her black-tipped tail, she sprang to join her companions.

"I put your stuff in the dryer," Lola says, coming into the kitchen.

"Thanks."

I had forgotten that I put a load of wash in last night. I'm absent-minded these days. How long would a load like that sit mildewing in the washer without Lola around?

Saturday night. Lola has finished packing her duffle bag with sports gear, plus a few items of clothing and, at my urging, some pens and paper. She sits at the kitchen table, eating a bowl of ramen noodles, even though we just finished a chicken dinner. Her phone beeps, she reads the new text message.

"Hey, Mom, Stef and Katie say they'll drive me to the airport tomorrow. That's okay, isn't it?"

"I was looking forward to doing it."

"Your car is due for servicing. The light has been flashing for a month."

"The car will be fine. I'll take it in next week."

"But you're okay with the Stef and Katie plan? I won't see them until Christmas."

"Sure. I guess that will work. If that's what you want."

"Don't forget to book your car in next week. At least get the oil changed."

It shouldn't be a big deal whether I say goodbye to Lola at home or at the airport. She's young. Her friends are important. That's normal. Although, of course, I had imagined a huggy Hallmark scene, with me included, at the departure gate. Initially I had even imagined driving her across the country, a chummy mother and daughter road trip ending at the front door of the student residences. I could check out her new room, maybe leave an African violet and some vitamins on her desk. But no. I never suggested such a plan to Lola. And although some of her friends were leaving town with a firmly attached mother-appendage, she never suggested it to me.

I saw the doe again in mid-summer. It was a Sunday night, which I remember because Lola had gone out with friends for an after-dinner bike ride, though we had been trying to keep Sunday nights as a mother-daughter event for the past few years. I was deadheading my flowers. I must have been working quietly because four deer, noses twitching, came down the slope and right up to my pots. The doe with the tumour leaned into the pot beside me. Her lips reached past the trailing verbena and tugged at a geranium cluster. The growth on her chest, purplish and red, dragged across the edge of the pot. She ate all my Martha Washingtons, leaving only stems and foliage, then backed off the deck and headed across the yard to Brad's.

I phoned Brad.

"Have you seen the deer with the tumour?" I asked. "She's at your place now. Can't we do something about it?"

"I called Fish and Wildlife," he said.

"And?"

"They said nature isn't always pretty."

"But that tumour has grown to the size of a volleyball."

"It's horrible," Brad said. "Try not to look at it."

Sunday morning. five a.m. I wait with Lola in the kitchen. She has one earbud plugged in from her iPod. The other ear is politely left open in case I want to start a conversation. Oh, I desperately want to start a conversation. Where the hell are Stef and Katie? Why are they so late and irresponsible? No, I promised myself not to fuss or nag. That's not how I want this morning to go. Breathe deep. I look out my bay window, but it's too dark to see anything outside.

I flick on the computer, search "deer with tumour" and discover "a hydrocyst on the brisket develops as a response to a traumatic injury at the site." Hunters delivered the clearest information. "Shoot a deer with a hydrocyst," one blogger advised. "Put her out of her misery. The meat is safe to eat."

I switch to the airline website, departure times. If Lola misses this flight, she'll just have to get another. I can't exactly ask her dad to pay for that—especially since I've been sitting here watching the lateness transpire. Guilt by acquiescence.

"Should we make a plan B?" I ask.

"They'll be here," Lola says.

I start the kettle. Watch the water boil. Pour a pot of tea. Watch it steep. Try not to eavesdrop when Lola answers her cell phone.

After a brief conversation, Lola shuts her phone and pops it into the front pocket of her jeans.

She says, "Stef's brother took the car last night and never brought it home. Katie can't use her mom's this morning."

"They just realized all this now?"

"I guess so. Can you drive me?"

"We can do this," I say. "Code red."

"Copy code red," Lola says. "Go, go, go."

I grab my ex-husband's jean jacket from the closet, pull it over my sweater, which is over my pyjama top. I have my black yoga pants on, which Lola hates and refers to as "mommy Lycra." Not exactly the outfit I would have planned to wear at the airport.

We hustle Lola's huge duffle bag into my car.

"Should I drive?" she asks as she closes the hatch. "I'm faster."

"I'm driving," I say.

I let Lola out at the airport doors. Tell her to check herself in. I'll catch up. By the time I park and get to the departures area, I spot Lola strolling, as though she's in no rush at all, towards security and the gates.

"Lola!" I call, jogging to her.

"I'm all checked in," she says.

"Where's your knapsack?" I ask.

"I checked it with my duffle bag."

"With your money in it?"

"Oops. They were rushing me."

"And your bank card?"

"I made a mistake. How come it took you so long to park the car?"

"And your ID? Honey, what will you to use to board?"

Lola pats the back pocket of her jeans. "Driver's license. Still in there from last night. Wow. That's lucky, eh?"

"Some women carry a purse," I say. "Hurry."

We run together down the rest of the hall. There is no

line at security. Lola shows the guard her boarding pass, turns and gives me a quick kiss on the cheek.

"Bye, Mom. See you at Christmas."

"Wait a sec," I say.

"Mom, I gotta go." Her voice quavers.

"Here," I say. I shove a twenty-dollar bill in her hand. "Just in case."

"Thanks. Love you, Mom." She blinks a few times, then presses the sleeve of her hoodie across her eyes. "Sorry about the Stef and Katie thing."

I wait at security until I see that Lola's flight has departed, presumably with her on it since she has not reappeared. On the drive home, I'm feeling badly that I never properly said goodbye. I never offered any words of wisdom. And if her knapsack doesn't show up, twenty dollars isn't enough to help her at all. Twenty dollars. That was the best I could do?

As I round the last curve onto our street, I see my deer standing beside the culvert. There's no one behind me, certainly not this early on a Sunday, so I stop. The light is at the glowing dawn stage, and the doe looks ghostly as she raises her head and walks onto the road. When she is directly in front of the car she comes into focus. I see that her hydrocyst is the size and colour of a basketball. Always growing. Her inner legs are worn raw from rubbing against it. She stares at me with those big glassy eyes, then walks awkwardly to the other side of the road and into a patch of brush where several other deer are nibbling on alder leaves.

At home, I put the kettle on for tea. Lola's packing list

is on the kitchen table. I pick it up and hold it between my palms until the kettle whistles. I set the packing list back on the table, pour the hot water over the tea leaves, and feel quite certain that I have done the right thing by never telling Lola about my deer.

BUCKAROO DRIVE-THRU

No shoes. I should expect this sort of thing from Adrian. But I am so surprised that he has bothered to put on a suit, albeit ill-fitted and greenish, that I don't notice his navy feet until he points them out.

"Thought I'd get my shoes resoled," he says as we stand outside the restaurant.

Despite my good manners, I stare. He distracts my gaze by flipping the bottom of his tie from under his belt.

"Maybe I should take these off, save wearing them out." He hops forward while he removes a sock.

"It's less noticeable with them on," I offer.

Adrian stuffs both socks in his suit jacket pocket. "There. Refreshing, really." He opens the restaurant door and pushes through ahead of me.

Adrian and I sit in a booth. An enormous parrot swings

from a plastic perch above our table, another clutches the back of my seat, and another dangles upside down from the cord that controls the window blinds. Adrian suggested the restaurant. No, not a restaurant, they call this an eatery. How appropriate.

"What darling feet," the waitress says, pointing at Adrian's bare toes protruding from under the table, "but you better keep them out of sight. You know, no shirt, no shoes, no service."

Adrian wriggles his toes. His feet are like a toddler's. Fleshy, with toes that line up evenly. The waitress giggles, picks up our oversized menus and spins around to another table, flaunting her short, backless dress. Sure, her figure's okay, but she's dressed to serve canapés, not fries.

I met Adrian when I was looking for one of those foolish fortieth birthday shirts for a client's wife. Adrian owned the T-shirt print shop. I operate a catering business. Food and service. Mostly service. Done properly. Every once in a while, a client will ask for a favour as part of a special occasion. Could I find a Tarzan to sing happy anniversary? Could I fold the napkins into sailboats? Could I arrange for a karaoke machine? There are endless ways to cheapen an event.

"Puff ink looks best," Adrian had said, rubbing his stubby finger over a thick roll of ink on the sample fabric. So tacky. So suited to my client's wife.

"Lordy, lordy, look who's forty. That's good if you've got a picture," Adrian said, laying various T-shirts on the counter. I picked out an orange Beefy-T which shouted FORTY AND SPORTY. As Adrian shoved the shirt into a bag he said, "Your birthday?"

"For a client. I guarantee I will not be getting a Beefy-T for my own birthday."

"No? Well, take this." Into the bag he stuffed a black tank top that said "VIXEN" in metallic puff ink.

"Thank you, I couldn't possibly."

"Here. It's you."

Vixen. Whatever made him think of that? In puff ink.

The waitress leans around the swinging parrot to lay down my Reuben sandwich. She says, "My mother had a big toe that bent so far to the right she had to have her second toe surgically removed to make room for it."

Adrian nods sympathetically. "My mom," he confesses, pulling his mushroom burger closer, "has such a bad hammer toe that she has to cut holes in her slippers. And bunions, bunions the size of walnuts."

"Imagine that," the waitress says, with a faraway look that suggests she already is imagining Adrian's mother's deformed feet.

"Have you any Dijon?" I ask.

The waitress brings the mustard in a separate dish, just as I requested. I take a little mustard and open my sandwich. The corned beef, pink and grainy, flops there like a dismembered part. I close the sandwich, wish I could cover it with my napkin, but that would be rude.

About a week after the T-shirt store, I was in the vegetable section of the supermarket when someone yelled, "Hey, vixen lady."

It was Adrian. I was wearing a sweater set, not the VIXEN tank top. I was examining artichokes. I frequently buy artichokes, because I know how to eat them. Adrian walked up the aisle towards me, his sandals slapping with every step, his blond leg hair standing on end from the air-conditioning. He yanked a handful of grapes from the bin beside the artichokes.

"You never told me what you do." He popped dirty grapes into his mouth while I explained how I oversee a staff of twelve, how I train each of them in table service and general etiquette, how, on occasion, I also arrange for the food and clean-up, everything from pâté to port.

"What do you do with those things?" Adrian pointed at the artichokes.

"I steam them. Artichoke leaves must be eaten with the fingers, while the heart must be eaten with a knife and fork."

"Wow. I'd like to see that."

"Don't you like your sandwich?" Adrian asks as he props his elbows on the eatery table and bites into his mushroom burger.

"It's missing a few details." I watch an oily drip slide down Adrian's pinky.

Adrian takes one hand off his burger and picks up a spoon from the table.

"That's why I need your advice," he says, pointing the

spoon at me. "I've been thinking about setting up a drive-thru in the lot beside my shop. Hamburgers, fries, even corn dogs." The oily drip progresses down Adrian's wrist and slips behind his shirt cuff. Adrian sets the spoon down on the table. His bare foot bumps against my shoe. I imagine the warm smudge on my navy pump.

I have never worn sandals or open-toed shoes. My mother said they were coarse. Nothing ruins a look more than a couple of bare toes. Especially if they're painted. Which isn't to say that I don't take care of my feet. Pumice, foot lotions, filing and cuticle reduction every week. But nothing can change the fact that they are feet, that my toes are like long parfait spoons, that my nails, despite my pedicures, are already thickening and horning with age.

"You being in the service industry, and a detail person, I thought you might have a few ideas for me," Adrian continues.

"People who eat in their cars don't deserve service."

"Of course. Good point. But what if they did? I want to do it properly."

Outside the restaurant, Adrian reaches into his pocket, fumbles around his socks, and hands me a bright yellow business card.

"Think about it. Here's my new card. I've got a cell phone now."

While Adrian walks away I read: "ADRIAN'S PUFF INK and BULK MEAT."

One of Adrian's socks lies on the pavement, not far from

my shoe. With my thumb and forefinger I pick the sock up, wrap it in Kleenex, and tuck it in the side pouch of my purse.

At home that night I lay Adrian's sock on the kitchen table. I would've expected Adrian to be the red or argyle type. But, properly laundered, this sock is quite tasteful. Navy with tiny maroon triangles. I place Adrian's business card beside the sock and think about calling him. Maybe I should wait until I have some advice on his drive-thru. I roll the sock up as though it had a mate, turning the top back on itself. Then I carry it to my bedroom, open my dresser drawer, and carefully lay the sock beside my lavender-scented hosiery.

Before I call Adrian, he phones me to say he needs a consultation, that day, after work. I tell him that I go to my health club after work.

"Okey-dokey," he says, without an invitation, "meet you there."

I never waver from my workout. Being thin is so much more discreet than the alternative. Especially on a tall woman like myself. Of course, clothing helps as well. I wear navy suits, classics, no elasticized waists, no sheer blouses, no bare legs.

At the gym, Adrian wheezes as he pedals. "The thing is, I've decided that this drive-thru is for kids. The Buckaroo Drive-Thru. No cars, just bikes."

"You're joking."

"What's yours set at?" he gasps.

"Eight."

Adrian stabs a number two into the dash of his stationary bike. "I open at the beginning of summer holidays, so I gotta get moving on it," he says, straightening up and pulling his shirt over his head. Flesh folds over his grey cotton shorts. Adrian pulls the shirt until the neck is at his hairline. He lets it drop behind him, like a wig.

"Have you done all your ordering?" I ask, politely focusing my eyes on a skylight.

"All the hardware and beef products."

"Condiments?"

"You're good. I'll get some ketchup. That's a condiment, isn't it?" Adrian pulls the shirt completely off his head and sets it on the handlebars. His pedaling slows to a stop. "You do this much?"

"Every night I'm not working."

"What for?"

"Hey," the receptionist calls as I walk out of the health club, "do you know that roly-poly guy?"

"Business associate," I say.

"Well, he left his watch with me. Came in dressed in his workout gear, so I guess he didn't get a locker."

He had no intention of showering, I think, recalling the sweaty seams of his shorts.

"Is he single?" the receptionist asks. "He seems fun."

"I'll take it to him." I snatch the watch from her hand.

The route I take home from the gym is cluttered with fast food outlets. I'm still clutching Adrian's watch—a big, red-banded Mickey Mouse with Minnie zipping around as the second hand. This is the closest I've ever been to a Mickey Mouse watch. When I learned to tell time my parents gave me a silver ladies' Bulova. I pass the watch to my un-cramped hand and try to imagine a bicycle drive-thru. I don't even know how to ride a bike that's not fixed to the floor. By the time I convinced my parents that I needed a bike, they couldn't find a girl's style that was tall enough for me. And the only fast food I ever had was when my uncle stopped by our house.

My uncle usually showed up during school holidays. He had enormous eyebrows that pasted themselves on his forehead in hot weather. My father might have had the same eyebrows, but he trimmed them regularly. Whenever my uncle arrived, my mother would breathe thinly, through her nose. Perhaps because she disapproved of his sneakers. At his age, she would say. Or perhaps because he called me Maddy instead of Madeleine.

I turn off the main road and stop at a speaker.

"I would like the hamburger, please," I say, squeezing Adrian's watch.

"The Happy or the Double Slam?"

I hesitate. The watch dampens in my hands. "Happy, thank you."

A waft of fried air comes through the window with the loosely wrapped package. Before I can set the package on the passenger seat, a drop falls from the foil and leaves a wet circle on my lap. I pull forward and park beside a plastic picnic table. Taking several sheets of Kleenex from my purse, I sit down on the edge of the plastic bench-seat and unwrap the Happy. I will not eat in my car.

The hamburgers my uncle bought were big. Not like this little thing, which is the size of a veal medallion on a dinner roll. My uncle would get me root beer. Always one size bigger than I asked him for. Once, he said I could take the mug home. I kept hair clips in that mug for about a year; my mother called it grotesque. I'll have to tell Adrian to serve root beer. Big root beer.

When I get home, I strip down to my underwear, stuff my hamburger-smelling clothes in the wash and pull on my VIXEN T-shirt. I sit on the edge of my bed, a sleigh bed with an amaryllis print comforter, the only piece of furniture that isn't from my parents' old house. All the rest of my place is hand-rubbed Georgian. Even in my bedroom, the highboy, with Adrian's sock in the top drawer, and the night table, are thin-legged cherry wood. And there's a Chippendale chair against the wall. I set Adrian's watch on the night table, let it bask in the red glow of my clock radio while I scratch my bare feet on the carpet.

A month later, Adrian calls in the morning. He's so excited I think he's talking nonsense.

"A donkey?"

"Miniature donkeys," Adrian says. "Alice and Nitro. I rented them for the grand opening tomorrow. Come see."

"Now?"

"C'mon. You can test the root beer."

The Buckaroo Drive-Thru sits in the middle of a paved lot and is the size of a proper table for six. The roof is a giant white Stetson. The walls are red and white Hereford. The awnings are plastic, rawhide-look. Adrian should have consulted me on decor.

"Which one is Alice?" I ask as Adrian, holding two ropes, leads the donkeys toward me. From this angle, I can't tell the male from the female. They are both the size of Great Danes, with thin leather halters and tiny, sharp black hooves. Adrian points to the brown donkey with a yellow tag attached to a fluorescent necklace. The tag reminds me of Adrian's business card. Alice lowers herself onto her forelegs.

"No, no, no," Adrian says, pulling up on the rope. Alice rolls on her back in the dusty pavement, wriggles her white-lined ears.

"She keeps doing that."

"What's the yellow tag for?"

"To keep the flies away. Nitro didn't come with one. Guess the flies don't like him."

Nitro, a grey-and-white male, stands passively while Alice finishes her roll and stands to nibble at the hem of Adrian's shorts.

"Nitro seems better behaved," I offer as Adrian swats at Alice's black lips.

"The guy who dropped them off said Nitro was unpredictable. But I can't see it. Here, hold these ropes and I'll get your root beer."

Adrian steps into the door at the back of the drive-thru. I hear the gurgling sound of his pop dispenser. The gritty ropes lay slack in my hand. Alice walks closer to me and nudges her nose in my palm. The hair on the back of my neck bristles. Alice nudges insistently. I pat her once between her shoulders, where two dark lines of hair form a cross. Dust poofs around my hand, under my nails.

Nitro whistles through his nose for a moment, then raises his nostrils in the air, sniffs. He takes deeper sniffs, exposing his thick yellowed teeth. I touch him under his jaw where the bone is stiff, sharp. Like an ankle bone. He flicks his wispy black tail, eyes me. Alice walks away, pulls on her rope until I let her lead me to the wooden leg of Adrian's huge "Buckaroo Drive-Thru" sign. She cocks her head sideways and begins to gnaw on the wood. Nitro whistles again.

My uncle used to whistle when we were driving for hamburgers. It was a full, strong whistle that didn't need any accompaniment, but sometimes he'd ask me to whistle along with him. Once, when I was a teenager, he told me his first wife left him because she hated his whistling. I wanted to know specifics, what exactly had she said, what songs didn't she like, was whistling outside the car acceptable? Finally, he said it wasn't the whistling, it was just bad sex. He whistled a bit more, then stopped to raise his eyebrows and say, "Don't tell your parents I used the 's' word."

My parents had me late in life and devoted themselves to teaching me etiquette. The movement of your soup spoon should always be away from you, corn niblets must be taken off the cob with your dinner knife, never dip your napkin in a finger bowl. Even back then, I realized some of the things they taught me were obsolete: when to use a footed wineglass, which side of a lady a man should walk on, how to properly tuck up the hand portion of a long glove during a formal dinner (and thereby leave the arm flesh modestly covered).

Adrian takes the ropes back and hands me a plastic mug of root beer.

"Did you know, if you don't trim their hooves they keep growing, out and up, like a big soup spoon?"

"A gravy ladle?"

"Exactly." Adrian picks yellow crust from the corner of Alice's eye, wipes his fingers on his shorts. "That's why I need you at the opening tomorrow. You know that kind of stuff."

I look down at the root beer, say, "Okay. Just the grand opening."

When I arrive for the opening, Alice and Nitro are nuzzling a bale of hay. Adrian has removed Alice's fluorescent collar and tied red bandannas around both the donkeys' necks. Adrian wears high-heeled cowboy boots and a giant silver belt buckle engraved "BUCKAROO." His cowboy boots are wide, but from the way his insteps are pushing at the leather I can tell they're not wide enough. He turns around to check the donkeys' halters and ropes and I get a good view of his Wranglers. They make his backside look like a cheese platter.

"C'mon in," Adrian motions to the door.

I step in before I realize how close together we'll be.

"Shut the door, bad manners to see the kitchen, eh?" he says. Adrian pushes a three-legged milking stool at me. "Have a seat. Put in one of those cassettes."

I stick a generic-looking tape in the player and quickly turn down the volume. Country twang for children, hardly dinner music. Adrian motions for me to turn it up. And up. Until the drive-thru throbs with ukuleles and giddy-ups.

Adrian heats up the grill and slices buns. Every time he turns from the little bit of counter on the right to the gas grill on the left, his belt buckle catches in the middle on the serving window. After reattaching the belt several times, he yanks on the buckle and zips the entire belt off his jeans.

"Can you find a place for this?" he shouts, handing me the belt and buckle while he lays a few burgers and frozen corn dogs on the grill and looks for his first customer.

Through the front window, I see two boys speed up to the drive-thru on their bikes. They stand up on the pedals and slam on their brakes just under the service ledge. Ball caps, untucked shirts, baggy jeans. How did they get by their parents in those clothes? I lean forward, listen.

"Yeehah, buckaroos!" Adrian yells. "What'll it be?"

"Are those real donkeys?" one boy asks.

"You bet your ass," Adrian laughs, and turns to give me a wink.

"Well they're fucking," the boy says, "and I'll have a corn dog."

Adrian squeezes by me and out of the drive-thru. I peer around the open door. A circle of children on bikes, skateboards, rollerblades, forms around the donkeys and

Adrian. Alice bucks, kicks out her hind legs. Nitro's hooves claw on the pavement as he jerks back a few steps, then lurches forward to mount her again. Alice bucks, Nitro bites at the sides of her lower neck. Alice swings her head from side to side, bares her big teeth and thin tongue. Adrian waves his hands and prances around the donkeys. He reaches for Alice's halter, gets nipped on the arm by Nitro. The cassette clicks to an end and I hear Alice and Nitro braying like rusty water pumps, Adrian yelling, "Get off her, she doesn't want it." I touch my face, feel the rising flush in my cheeks, sense a sweaty dampness in my navy pumps.

"My corn dog?" the kid at the window complains.

I hurry to the grill, lift off a corn dog, wrap a Kleenex around the base of the stick to serve as a napkin, and hand it to him with a smile. My mother's smile. The same smile she gave my uncle whenever he gave her bottom a friendly pat or tried to massage her shoulders. The close-lipped smile that said, "You are barely tolerable." I swore I would never use that smile, but in fact, I have found it very useful in my day-to-day business.

"Would you like some root beer?" I ask as the boy hands me his money and squeals around the corner to watch the donkeys.

I look out the door again. Nitro has dismounted. Adrian leads Alice out of the circle of spectators, talks to her, gently touches the bite marks on her neck. Alice pauses, urinates on the pavement. The glistening pool spreads under her hooves, under the soles of Adrian's cowboy boots, and drives the crowd towards the order window.

Adrian has big sweat circles and grease spots on his shirt. He has come close to frying his stomach several times, especially during the rush of business after the donkey event. But now, in the early afternoon, the customers have thinned. We have not discussed the donkeys. At my own suggestion, I have been keeping track of the number of customers, what they ordered, their approximate age (a wild guess there), and their comments. Occasionally, at Adrian's request, I hand him a bag of buns or a tomato. Sometimes I take a basket of cut potatoes out of the fryer.

"I should be going," I say. "I have to work tonight."

"I'm sorry if the donkeys offended you." Adrian quickly pulls hot dog links out of a box. "I didn't want that."

"I didn't pay any attention." I set my clipboard down on a bag of onions. "Here's the numbers, they should help with your orders in the future. You'll want to put napkins on your list. And perhaps some red relish as an alternative to green."

"Good idea."

Alice, tied up on the other side of the lot, gnaws at the Buckaroo sign. Nitro, standing in the shade of the giant Stetson and tied to the condiment counter, shuffles slightly towards me as I step out of the doorway. His sides expand like bellows, he whistles, then throws back his head and brays and brays and brays.

"Forgot my purse," I say as I reach back into the drive-thru. Adrian, now cutting hot dog links, nods but does not look. I grab his belt from under the stool and hurry to my car.

Late that night, when I get home from supervising my staff at a cocktail event, I slip into my VIXEN shirt. My feet are cramped and swollen from standing in leather pumps, so I sit on the edge of the bed and massage them with both hands. It's time for my weekly pedicure but, for once, I can't motivate myself. Instead, I check the sock in my lingerie drawer and readjust the Mickey Mouse watch on my bedside table. The BUCKAROO belt dangles on the closet doorknob.

I fold back the comforter, lie on the bed, and wiggle my long, rough toes towards the ceiling. Flexing my feet, I stretch my calves and thighs before moving my legs in a bicycle motion. When my legs tire, I pause, pull my underwear to my toes. With a punch of my feet, I donkey-kick the underwear into the air, watch them land on the tapestried seat of the Chippendale chair. Adrian's pants, perhaps his Wranglers, perhaps his greenish suit pants, will hang nicely over the elegant arm of that chair.

STILL MAKING TIME

Labour Day weekend. Scott stops on the bluff above the canoe club. He dismounts, leans his bike against the metal arm of the bench seat. After unbuckling and removing his helmet, hanging it on the handlebars, he pulls his cell phone out of the back pocket of his cycling jacket.

He unlocks the screen. Pauses.

No, he won't call her.

Nadia is staying at her parents' house, helping them pack before they move into a condo. One step before the grave, her father keeps saying. Her mother thwacks him on the back, then kisses him, then says moving is the smart thing to do at their age. Nadia's kids are spread throughout the house. The two youngest are upstairs taking turns playing on the computer. The two oldest—teenagers—are in the basement with her and have found a stack of warped vinyl records. She can hear them guffawing their way through each album cover.

Nadia kneels, opens a cardboard box full of outdoor gear from her job at the canoe club. She had boxed the gear up twenty years ago on the pretence that she might use it again. But even back then she knew she was done paddling; she was storing Scott away.

She takes out her fluorescent pink ball cap and her navy cagoule rain jacket. Nadia didn't mind paddling in the rain. The kids she taught didn't mind either. And Scott didn't mind. When they went for a paddle after work, he let the rain run over his head and face, down his neck. He'd be in his soaking T-shirt and shorts, water dripping off his elbow with the recovery part of each stroke, and he'd be smiling like the sun shone for him each day.

Nadia hears her cell phone ringing, supposes it is her husband calling from Vancouver. Catching a flight today, joining them for the weekend to help with the move. Then everyone back to Vancouver for work and the start of school—the end of the summer, the start of the rain. She stops that line of thought. She knows better than to compare the routine of twenty years of marriage to the heat of a summer fling.

Nadia doesn't go for her phone. She'll check her messages later. She pulls on her pink ball cap. Thinks about what Scott would look like now. He would have a middle-age crinkle in the corner of his eye, but he had that even when he was young, when he worked at the patrol hut. He would be slim, coordinated, like he was when she saw him on the bike path above the reservoir ten years ago. She only had Garth and Todd then, and Todd had just started school, and she was cranky with them for tugging her arms, for being impatient. Scott would be the kind of middle-aged man who still hopped on his bike every day, every season, to ride to work; who could still sit cross-legged while helping a kid with a bowline knot and be awed by an osprey snatching a northern pike from the water. His skin would be more leathered now, but he would still have an expression that announced he was not a cynic. Happy, the way he looked when she saw him on the bike path. But he had always looked like that.

Scott sits on the bench, looks across to the patrol hut, shakes his head. He shouldn't have stopped here. It makes him feel like some rube who can't move on, like he wishes he was still twenty-four and working on the patrol and rescue boat. Pathetic. Because for all his first-responder courses, and water rescue training, and experience in jet boats and sailboats, for coming all the way from Muskoka, the job hadn't required much more than putting around the reservoir. The patrol boat was the only jet boat allowed on the water, so there was some status attached to being in it, but driving slowly with that powerful engine always seemed like a waste. Sometimes he towed a canoe or sailboat back to shore. Mostly he drove around telling people not to swim in the water. He met Nadia on a Friday, which meant regatta day for all the canoe and sailboat camps on the water. He and Eddy—he was always on a shift with Eddy—spotted a group of kids standing in their canoes. One kid at the stern of each canoe, right up on the gunwales, bending their knees, swinging their arms, bobbing a crooked track across the reservoir. A swimming incident waiting to happen, Eddy figured.

Nadia was their instructor, gunwale-bobbing her own canoe. When they pulled the motorboat beside her, she crossed her arms and continued to stand with a foot on either gunwale. She was all lean legs in short shorts, sporting a Neoprene PFD as opposed to the heavy Mae West lifejackets the kids had to wear, and a fluorescent pink ball cap—all the instructors wore a hat that kids could easily spot on the water—and black hair tied in a low ponytail. Eddy gave her the lecture on swimming in the reservoir— how there was a by-law against it since it was the city's drinking water, and how, anyway, the water was glacially cold. Downright dangerous, especially if a kid conked his head on the canoe on the way in. Nadia looked around, said she didn't see anyone swimming. Nadia wasn't the type to be intimidated by guys like Eddy, with cut-off shirts and fire-hydrant arms.

Eddy was mad. Scott said they should relax the rule. It was summer; it wasn't that big a deal if kids fell in. Eddy said the water could be seriously fouled because there were so many of them; worse, gunwale-bobbing would become a habit. Scott said he'd bike by the canoe club on his way home and talk with her. Eddy raised his eyebrows, said okay, he got the drift.

When Scott got to the canoe club, Nadia was working

on a pile of life jackets, moving them from a heap on the ground to the pegs on the wall. Scott asked if he could have a canoe lesson. She said she only taught kids. He said, if you give me lesson I'll keep Eddy off your case all summer. She said she'd rather trade for a water ski behind the patrol boat, but since that would cost them both their jobs, she'd teach him the canoe strokes—the J, the draws and sweeps, the braces—in exchange for help with hanging the jackets.

He remembers the tone of her arm, the quietness of her laugh.

Scott looks at the cell phone in his hand. Of course he won't call her. He only has her parents' home phone number, memorable even though he hasn't dialed it in twenty years. She lived with her parents that summer. Surely they've moved. Maybe they've died.

Scott has seen Nadia only twice in the twenty years since that summer. Once when he was riding his bike to work, he saw her walking with kids near the canoe club. Even though she'd cut her hair he knew her right away—she came up on her toes with each step, light, ready to spring, the same way she walked down the dock—with or without a canoe on her shoulders. He stopped his bike. She introduced her kids. He can't remember their names; there were two, and one looked more like her than the other. She was in town visiting her parents. The kids complained about being cold; the bigger one asked if their dad was going to the movie with them that night. That was about it.

A few years later, he saw her at the Stampede. He was with his crew from the fire hall. They were all going to the chuckwagon races, then to Dusty's, where the guys would always try and fix him up with a woman they just happened to know and who just happened to be there. Nadia was at the Stampede water ride, climbing into the front seat of a fake hollowed-out log. A little jean skirt, same great legs, shifting to one side as she hoisted her youngest child onto the log ahead of her. It seemed like she had four kids with her, a range of ages. That surprised him. Four kids now. Scott had tugged the brim of his cowboy hat down and walked by. He had not married or had children and that day at the Stampede he had somehow felt less the man for it. He was in his forties now, wiser, and well past that feeling.

Nadia pulls her old white Converse sneakers out of the box. With their rubber toes and the little holes at the arches that allowed the water to drain out, they were the ideal canoeing shoe. She wore them every day at work and on the night paddles with Scott. She remembers the soft dip and gurgle as she and Scott paddled up to the river mouth at the head of the reservoir, and then the gentle pull of the current after they tied their canoes together under the footbridge, lay down beside a low campfire on the riverbank, listened for the *kroo-oo* of an owl.

Inside one of the runners, wrapped in a fuzzy hair elastic, is a stack of cards, one card for each paddling certification. The courses were taught by the commodore of the canoe club. He was a garrulous, big-bellied Brit who, like Scott, was in a perpetual good mood. He and his wife owned a convenience store. They worked the same shifts at the store so they could be together. That season, the commodore had hardly been out at all in his own canoe. When he came down one night during the last week of summer, Scott, who was there waiting for Nadia to finish work, asked if he needed a hand carrying his cedar strip down to the dock. The commodore said thank you, thank you, but he'd been carrying a canoe for longer than Scott had been alive.

It had been raining a lot and the dock was slippery. The commodore put his boat in the water, tied it to the ring. Then he went back to his car to help his wife down to the shoreline. She never went in the boat with him—she had frail, spidery legs and used two canes—but she sat on the shore in a fold-out lawn chair, reading, waving, while he canoed back and forth in front of her. After the commodore set her up that day, after they kissed, as he was returning to his canoe on the dock, he slipped. He let out a great whoop and his feet flew up in front of him. It was funny at first—a man with a big belly doing a banana-peel fall into the water. "Tell him swimming is illegal," someone said, and that brought a laugh from everyone on shore, even from the commodore's wife.

It was a long time before the commodore surfaced. Scott hurried to the dock. Nadia followed. The commodore's bald head rose out of the water. He spluttered, then his arms began flapping. He didn't appear to be a very good swimmer, but he was making progress and he didn't have far to go. His hands lunged at the dock. Scott hauled him onto the boards, rolled him on his back. The commodore stopped gasping. Call 911, Scott said, taking the commodore's pulse with two fingers.

Nadia remembers running up the dock toward the phone in the club. At the end of the dock she noticed the commodore's wife—hands locked onto the arms of the lawn chair, neck muscles taut and white, eyes devastated, utterly devastated. Later, when Nadia played the scene back, again and again, she didn't think much about the commodore, she focused on his wife. How could the commodore's wife possibly bear losing a love like that?

From his bench above the reservoir, Scott sees the patrol boat docked across the water. Still an open-bow jet boat, good for shallows and travelling upstream. The only time he was in it alone was the last day of that summer. Labour Day weekend. It was dark when he took the keys from the hut and slowly crossed the reservoir at six a.m. He could see Nadia walking down the canoe club dock with a ski under her arm. Her head was bare; she wore a shorty wetsuit. He pulled the boat up and handed her the rope, a new one. Back then he didn't know anyone in the city who could loan him a ski rope. She had told him she liked the rope twenty-eight feet shorter than the standard seventy-five, so he knew she was going to be good.

He doesn't remember her jump-start off the dock, or even her first few turns, he only remembers her rhythm once she settled in, the spray from her ski as she cut one turn after another, the empty water ahead of the boat. After looping the reservoir, he tucked in close to shore so she could release the rope handle and ride her ski into the shallows. The water was only up to her knees when she stopped.

No swimming involved, he joked when he pulled the boat up, tossed her a towel. Then he noticed she was crying. He asked if she'd hurt herself. She tightened the towel around her shoulders, said no, thanks, everything was perfect.

Not exactly perfect. It was nothing about him, she said, but she was going to leave him right after the weekend. She was headed to BC to find work as a lifeguard in Vancouver. There were plenty of lifeguard jobs in Calgary so he knew, he knows, her leaving was all about him.

Nadia has slipped a Converse sneaker onto her hand. The white rubber toe has grey streaks on it from the aluminum Grumman canoes she used when teaching. She slides the shoe on the floor beside her, back and forth, a slalom run on the carpet. Labour Day weekend. She remembers him coming to pick her up that last morning, an apparition driving out of the mist in the white boat. He wasn't wearing a patrol jacket—he was wearing a blue hoodie with the hood over his head. And when he handed her the rope at the dock, he had the calmest expression in his eyes. Just here we go. Before the rope tightened he pushed down his hood. And when she was skiing, she could see the shape of his back muscles under his hoodie, the back of his head, his shaggy hair, his thumbs-up when he turned to watch her. The water, the morning, the summer. The guy. She never wanted them to lose their pre-dawn shimmer.

Nadia pulls her hand out of the sneaker, leans back against the basement wall, hears the constant lap of the boat wake against the shore in front of the canoe club, pictures Scott leaning toward her with a green towel in his hands, the start of a smile on his face as though he's about to make a joke. Then she hears her two younger kids upstairs sliding furniture, maybe trying to reach for something too high, or making a fortress. She hears the two teenagers in the next room planning to build a ceiling-high pyramid with her old album covers. That will never work, Nadia thinks. She takes off her ball cap, goes up to make everyone a snack.

Scott tucks his cell phone into the pocket of his cycling jacket. He stands and looks at the full length of the canoe club dock below him. He thinks about the commodore dying there, about how the commodore's wife phoned the patrol hut a few days after the death and thanked Scott for his efforts. She had been on the shore, watching him perform his first responder duties, his unstopping CPR. She said she was grateful for the commodore, for their time together. She said she'd had more than her share of happiness, that every day with the commodore had been a treasure.

Scott reaches for his helmet. It's time to go home.

PUBLICATION HISTORY

"Basic Obedience"
The New Quarterly. Winter 2012.

"Still Making Time"
The Prairie Journal. Fall 2011.

"Eulogy for the Feminist Movement"
Other Voices. Fall 2011.

"Breaking the Mould"
FreeFall. Fall 2011.

"Mrs. Goodfellow's Dog"
Grain. 2008.

"Western Taxidermy"
Alberta Views. 2007.

"Big Fork Campground"
The Dalhousie Review. 2007.

"My Brother's Shit-kickers"
Alberta Views. 2003.

"Thanksgiving" (published as "Stanley's Wish")
Yalobusha Review. 1999.

"Buckaroo Drive-Thru"
Other Voices. 1997.

ACKNOWLEDGEMENTS

Many thanks to Anne Nothof, editor extraordinaire, and to all the readers, writers, friends, and neighbours who have provided feedback and fact-checks over the years.

Love and appreciation always to Mike, Ross, and Stu.

ABOUT THE AUTHOR

Barb Howard is a third-generation Calgarian who worked as a lawyer and a land contract analyst before receiving her M.A. in Creative Writing from the University of Calgary. In 2009, Barb received the Writers' Guild of Alberta (Howard O'Hagan) Award for short fiction. She has won contests in *Alberta Views* and *Canadian Lawyer*, and was a finalist at the Western Magazine Awards.

Barb's first novel, *Whipstock*, was published by NeWest Press in 2001. Since then, Barb has published the novella *Notes for Monday* (Recliner, 2009), and the young adult novel *The Dewpoint Show* (Fitzhenry & Whiteside, 2010). Barb lives in Bragg Creek, Alberta with her husband, a pair of easygoing sons, and one neurotic dog.

TELL THE WORLD
THIS BOOK WAS

Good	Bad	So-so